The Ring Bearer

Book 6 of
THE WARDEN

Felicia Jedlicka

For those who make mistakes.

SISTER WITCHES
THE DEVIL'S SHADOW
THE DEVIL'S SOUL

DESTINY REJECTED
DESTINY RECLAIMED
DESTINY RAZED
DESTINY RESTORED

DÉJÀ VU

SAVE THE HUMANS

THE NECROMANCER'S CHILD

THE NEBRASKA APOCALYPSE NOVELS
CORN COWS AND THE APOCALYPSE
COW TIPPING AFTER THE APOCALYPSE
CORN HUSKING AFTER THE APOCALYPSE

THE WARDEN SERIES
SUCCESSORS
RIVALS
LOVERS AND LIARS
BAD BLOOD
TENANTS AND TYRANTS
THE RING BEARER
GODS AND MONSTERS
BEASTS AND BURDENS
MAGIC AND MAYHEM
FORK IN THE ROAD
DETAILS AND DEADLINES
*CURSES AND SACRIFICES**
*WITCHES AND WOLVES**
*SAINTS AND SERPENTS**
*ENEMIES AND ALLIES**

MARRIED TO DEATH*

THE RING BEARER

FELICIA JEDLICKA

1

DANATO LET THE DOOR to his office slam into the wall. The seemingly indestructible glass rattled loudly. Ethan unloaded his firearm into the bin beside the door, as he always did. The three men who accompanied General Clark to the late-night—or rather, early-morning—meeting, made no attempts to offer up their weapons.

"Put your guns in the bin," Danato instructed impatiently midway to his desk.

General Clark smirked innocently. "Really, Danato, I don't think all that is necessary. We are all gentlemen here. I think we can keep our tempers in check enough not to shoot each other."

Danato had never had much cause to associate with General Clark, but the little he knew of him he didn't like. Clark was a typical high-ranking military officer who assumed that he owned every situation simply by wearing a uniform. Conversely, Clark knew little of Danato and even less about the importance of his rules. "Given what I've heard this evening, I'm not so sure about that, but suit yourself." Danato gave Ethan a stern glance that would hopefully make him stand down without a verbal order. He didn't want to appear at odds with his successor in front of Clark. Ethan was no doubt struggling with his decision to let Cori be arrested and detained, but so far, he was still obeying him.

Danato headed to his chair, and Ethan took position against the wall like a stone statue. One of Clark's soldier drones entered the room with his gun still firmly holstered. He looked as smug as his commander, no doubt pleased that he could keep his weapon in hand. Men like that had the skill to use a firearm, but they lacked deference for its power. To them, it was just an extension of their cock. They didn't have any intimate understanding of its consequences.

Danato was certainly not anti-gun. Every guard in his prison was well armed. He just no longer saw any reason for a man of his stature and temperament to be holding a device that could kill with the flick of his finger. Most of his staff already quaked in their boots at his presence. He didn't want them pissing themselves as well.

Danato felt the air cool instantly in the room. He couldn't suppress a smile at the change in the soldier's demeanor. His prideful gleam melted into befuddled concern. He let out a solemn yelp before his body was hurled backward, disrupting his compatriots, who were entering behind him. His impromptu flight landed on the general, flattening him to the floor.

Ethan was doing his best to maintain his stern soldier-like exterior, especially with real soldiers present, but Danato knew he was shocked by the event. He had never explained to Ethan or Cori why they couldn't bring weapons into the office. He didn't believe in long-winded explanations regarding his orders. Either you follow them or you don't. It doesn't matter if you understand them.

Clark offered Danato a glower as he got back to his feet, combing down his nonexistent hair before returning his beret. "You might have clarified the reasoning behind your request."

"I don't make requests. I give orders, and I *don't* repeat myself."

Clark clearly didn't want to offer any concessions to Danato, but the soldiers grudgingly deposited their weapons in the door-side bin without any further instruction. Clark was the last to remove his. After doing so, he offered a nod to Danato like he was bestowing the action on him in good faith instead of just bending to his authority.

As Danato sat down, he noticed the bottom drawer of his desk stuck out further than the others. He reached to pull on the drawer, but found it locked despite the slight protrusion. It was a stiff drawer, difficult to open and difficult to close, especially since he hadn't opened it in a good number of years.

A thought crossed his mind that he hoped to disprove. He pulled open his center drawer and searched the tiny compartments holding paper clips, tacks, pencils, and his drawer key. When it was not there, he searched the far back of the drawer, just in case. The key was gone. He shoved the center drawer closed, wondering and, at the same time, knowing how much Cori now knew.

"Something wrong?" Clark said, patiently waiting for Danato to speak. His men stood behind and on either side of him. It was all a nice show of dominance, but Danato only sucked up to paper-pushing bureaucrats who intended to give him money. General Clark would get nowhere flaunting his authority here, because he had none. Not in this country, not in this prison, and certainly not in this room.

Danato looked at Ethan. "My key," he murmured to see if his face would change. Ethan's brow dipped nearly indiscernibly, as if he were trying to interpret the meaning of the secret code word.

"Shall I get you a screwdriver?" Clark offered, with more than a spoonful of amusement in his eyes.

"That won't be necessary." Danato reached down and ripped open the lower drawer. The metal tab designed to prevent invasion pinged against the bottom of the drawer along with the lock it held.

He stared at the files lying before him. He felt a thousand memories trample over his *here and now,* with muddy footprints from the past. He pulled out the ones he needed, leaving the red marked one in the drawer. His leg hurt just looking at the dreaded thing. He slammed the drawer shut, and hoped this time the action would still his thoughts and ease his pain. Unfortunately, the drawer was still just a drawer, and had no magical powers to induce amnesia.

Belus arrived late, mercifully breaking him from his unwelcome reverie. Danato had called him shortly after Cori's arrest, to give him the rough draft by phone. It only took the mention of Cori being in trouble to prompt a long sigh from him. Danato could hear him shuffling in search of pants even before he explained the situation. After the overview of the night, he didn't say much. Belus was always more level-headed than him, but Danato got the distinct impression that he was just as disappointed by Cori's lack of protocol as he himself was.

Instead of his usual obscure position on the file cabinet, Belus positioned himself on the opposite side of the desk across from Ethan. It offered a nice balance of power to counter Clark's triad of strength.

"Gentlemen." Belus nodded to the men respectfully. Danato couldn't bring himself to offer anything but a cold stare. Belus reached across the desk for the elemental files. He yawned before beginning his cursory read. It impressed Danato that he could stay calm even with the elementals out of their cages and Cori in one. Not because he thought for one second that Belus was actually unruffled by the incident, but because he was such a good actor when it really counted.

"What exactly are we waiting for, Danato?" Clark rolled his eyes at Belus's studies. "Aren't you going to send your collectors to get my prisoners back?"

"I will when I'm satisfied that our documentation is up to my standards." Danato leaned back in his chair, tenting his fingers over his chest. He wouldn't mention that the second phone call he'd made after Cori left was to release the collectors.

He was certain the only reason Cori released the elementals was because she'd honestly felt their lives were in danger. Her previous encounter with Efrat, albeit still confusing to him, revolved around one basic principle: she didn't want anyone to get shot, and that included Efrat.

Danato never quite understood why she had so much sympathy for a man who had tried to kill her, but Cori's natural instincts were to preserve life. He imagined the death of her mother and her aunt had left her with a strong desire to avoid further death. Friend or not, she didn't want anyone in her life to die. It wasn't a bad trait per se, but her reverence for life was apparently interfering with the basic purpose of his prison: to contain prisoners.

Danato may not have agreed with her method of protection, but if she was willing to violate the cardinal rules to save them, then the least he could do was not put them right back into the lion's mouth.

"The documentation was up to your standards when you signed it six years ago," Clark pointed out, mimicking Danato's tranquil behavior by leaning back in his own chair. Neither of them looked as composed as Belus, but they did their best between volleyed cold stares.

"I may have missed something," Danato pointed out.

"You still signed it," Clark snapped.

"And you signed our contracts," Belus interrupted. "Why don't you tell us what happened with Cori? Did she assault you and your men? And if so, how did a woman dressed in a full-length evening gown and high heels get the drop on you?" Belus said it with utter dullness, but Danato knew he was just taking his shots as he could get them. Danato was glad for it. Belus always knew the best ways to get under people's skin without outright insulting them.

"She released some kind of weather device on us." Danato caught the glance that Belus gave him. They were both thinking the same thing. *What weather device?* "According to the inscription on the container," Clark continued, "it was the Spirit of Pamola." Danato did his best not to show his grievance to this, but he couldn't help but grind his teeth. Belus offered him a glance that hinted at the irritation he had thus far been hiding.

"How did she break it?" Belus turned back to Clark, abruptly losing his muted ire in exchange for curiosity.

"Efrat helped her. He was helping her the whole time, protecting her. If you ask me, I think they had this planned for a while. They looked quite cozy together, her ensconced in his arms while he defended her." Clark didn't offer Ethan any specific look, but it was clearly meant for him. Ethan maintained his indifferent façade, but his breathing hastened.

"What exactly did she need defending from, General?" Danato asked.

"Well, you didn't think I was just going to let her attack us?" Clark scoffed.

"So, you were up in arms against a seemingly defenseless woman?" Danato tipped his head. "I mean, you didn't know what the snow globe could do, so why did she need protection by Efrat?"

Clark said nothing.

"I can only make assumptions as to what defenses Efrat must have offered her, and I assure you if those defenses had failed, and she was hurt in any way by your men, we would not be conversing right now... because you would be dead."

"Now, now, Danato, the top floor is my territory."

Danato smiled and let out a laugh that puzzled everyone in the room. "General, before we continue with this conversation, it is very important that you understand what a valued tenant you are to me. Your contributions to our facility have been vital to maintaining a clean and safe environment for our prisoners and our wards. However, that aside, let me assure you that every inch of this prison belongs to me." Danato and Clark maintained a short standoff before Belus interrupted.

"Tell us about this unarmed woman you shot," Belus said, indifferent to the flagging egos in the room.

"Dr. Jillian Frank was threatening to shoot one of my prisoners," Clark said flatly.

Danato knew of the woman in question; she was a singer hired to provide entertainment for last night's party, a party that had been a present for Cori. He didn't know the woman personally, and as far as he knew, neither did Cori. Yet, she'd seemed to have intimate knowledge of her when Clark came to arrest her.

He couldn't imagine that Cori had enough time to get the woman's life story before the incident, let alone get into his files. Something about the timeline of Cori's night wasn't adding up, and he wanted to know what it was.

"You did know her then?" Belus asked.

"Yes, she was the doctor that treated my prisoners prior to our relocation." Clark answered the question dutifully, but kept his eyes on Danato rather than Belus. Like most military men, he preferred to speak to the senior officer. Even if Danato had the foresight to ask all the right questions, he still preferred Belus to take the reins so he could watch Clark wobble on his self-built pedestal.

"Cori said the doctor created them. How does one create elementals?" Danato offered the question to Belus just as much as Clark.

"That's classified," Clark said—the standard political avoidance.

"It says here," Belus interjected again, "that you were forced to contain the elementals due to volatile potential and issues of aggression, but it doesn't actually say what they did."

"That's also classified," Clark repeated.

Belus was about to object, but Danato was already on top of it. "Bullshit it is. Any prisoner housed in this facility has to have a detailed file. We need to know their issues of aggression and their volatile potential."

"Is this really all because of the girl?" Clark changed the subject. "She committed a crime. I'm not going to give her a slap on the wrist and let her go. If you expect leniency from me, then you'd better get my prisoners back."

"Cori doesn't break rules for no reason," Belus argued, a little more vehemently than Danato would have expected, considering he liked to keep his emotions out of his job. "If she let your prisoners go, she must have seen something that caused her to believe they were being unlawfully held. Why don't you just skip this need-to-know crap? She will tell us anyway."

"I don't think so, gentlemen. She's in my custody now. Unless my prisoners are returned to me soon, the bitch is going to an American prison, where she'll stay."

Ethan lost his queen's guard composure and stepped toward the general. "Watch your mouth!"

The nearest soldier intercepted him and pushed him back against the wall, hard. "Stand down, boy!" The soldier was several inches taller than Ethan. It probably made him feel superior. He also had about twenty pounds of muscle working for him, but that didn't stop Ethan.

Somewhere between them busting into the house, Clark insulting his wife, and this guy calling him *boy*, Ethan had met his limit on stoic obedience. He grabbed the soldier's neck and slammed his face down into Danato's desk. Blood dribbled out onto the gray metal top, but Ethan didn't let him get back up. To prove his point, he held the man's head down with one hand. The soldier grunted and struggled, but he was powerless under Ethan's dragon-grown muscles.

Ethan rarely flaunted his strength, which was best, since he preferred to be a leader in the trenches instead of a leader on high. At that moment, though, Danato knew he was proud that he could best another man without breaking a sweat.

One of the other soldiers moved to rescue his partner. "I wouldn't advise that. He does have two hands," Danato said.

"As I was saying," Clark said, ignoring Ethan, "the upper floor, though rented, houses my prisoners, not yours. They are my responsibility, and therefore, *any* threats against them or my men will be dealt with by me. She has stolen and released property of the United States of America, so she will be prosecuted in America."

This turn of threat surprised Danato. He'd expected Clark to use Cori as leverage to make sure he got his property back, but at the moment, he seemed more concerned about punishing Cori than the risk of his escaped elementals. The general should have been an easy man to read since he was a walking, talking ball of harvested pride, but he wasn't probing Danato's anger for his amusement. He was establishing his rights to carry out his plans, which left the remaining question: Why would Clark want to take Cori back to America?

Ethan released his prey. "That can't be," he seethed, misinterpreting Danato's silence as acquiescence.

"It won't be," Danato assured him, without any ire in his tone. "*As I was saying*, every inch of this prison belongs to me. That includes Cori. She is not just another employee doled out by overcrowded prisons. She's a slave. Purchased property, registered with my corporate headquarters. If you even attempt to extradite her for this, *you* would be stealing."

Clark chuckled, looking at something of no consequence on the floor.

"Something you find particularly amusing?" Danato asked.

"This conversation." Clark eyed Belus as if his presence were suddenly offending him. Belus peeked over the file at him, but didn't waste his energy to glare back at him. "We're discussing legal guidelines for an illegal operation. It's like trying to get workman's comp for burglars injured during a bank robbery." Clark pulled a handkerchief out of his pants pocket and handed it to his man with the bleeding nose. "I don't really think that theft of a slave would be considered a crime where I come from."

"If that's the way you want to go, we'll just forget about what I signed and you can vacate the premises on the next available truck. You can find your own prisoners and I'll deal with Cori," Danato said.

"You would lose a good deal of income without my prisoners."

"That would be a shame, but I'm sure I would manage."

Clark sighed. "I was hoping this meeting was going to be productive, but it appears that the wee hours of the morning have made you cranky. My men are due for a break, anyway." Clark stood, flattening his uniform despite the fact that his rounded belly had long since prevented him from looking regal in it. "I'll make a deal with you—no contracts or signatures. Just bring back my prisoners and I will release the woman." Clark smiled like he expected Danato to believe he was offering a worthy solution out of the goodness of his heart.

"As soon as I have the whole picture, I'll send out the collectors," Danato lied.

Clark raised an eyebrow at Danato's prevarication. "Very well, Danato. Until then, Cori will be safe, guarded by my men, to ensure a rapid solution to this... drama."

His lack of insistence baffled Danato. He was once again content to keep Cori as his prize until he got his prisoners back. It was troublesome, because Danato knew Clark was a very regimented man. Anything out of the ordinary, off schedule, or outside of his plans should have sent him into a panicked O.C.D. tantrum. Which begged another question: *Was* everything going according to his plans?

2

C LARK AND HIS MEN left, collecting their weapons on the way out. Danato looked at Belus and gave him a nod that hopefully expressed his gratitude. Belus exhaled like he was finally just feeling the frustration Danato had been feeling for the last few hours. He moved to a chair to sit comfortably while he finished reading the files.

Ethan danced around looking like he wanted to punch something, but since he knew it was best not to, he just continued to get more worked up. "I can't believe that guy," he finally spat.

"He's just doing what uptight American generals do." Danato knew that was little consolation, but he didn't want to further amp up Ethan's exasperation by agreeing with him.

"What? Exert authority where they have no business to?" Ethan asked sarcastically.

"Yes," Belus and Danato answered simultaneously.

"We need to talk to Cori," Belus continued, tossing the files back on Danato's desk. "Unless I missed something, there seems to be a big gap between Cori dancing happily ever after into the night and going against the cardinal rule of this prison."

"I agree. Her actions may have been based solely on preserving the elementals' lives, but I don't see how she went from barely trusting Efrat to risking her life to save him."

"She risked her life to save him before," Belus pointed out.

"No, she risked her life to save *you*," Danato corrected, which made Belus momentarily look away. "At any rate, I'm still surprised she didn't come to me right after Jill and Hirem were killed. She should have known I wouldn't tolerate that kind of action."

"She might have been suspicious that they were being held unjustly," Ethan said, putting his foot up on the vinyl chair. Danato didn't bother correcting him. They had more important things to deal with than manners. "After her incident with Efrat," Ethan continued, "she seemed off. She was asking about the elementals: who they were and why they had been put here. I told her as much as I knew. I thought she was satisfied with that."

"So, you had no idea she was going to do this?" Danato asked.

"Of course not," Ethan said, clearly disappointed that he would even ask.

"Do you know when she discovered the key to my drawer?" Danato asked.

"What key?" Ethan peered over the desk like he had never realized there was a bottom locked drawer. He shrugged. "I didn't even know there was anything in there. How do you know she..." Ethan stopped his attempt to help Cori evade the accusation. "Maybe she just stumbled onto to your key and got a little snoopy."

"Surmising isn't necessary. We just need to talk to her," Belus said. "They've got her held up on the part-time level. None of the cells on the top floor even lock anymore."

"I'll go talk to her." Ethan moved to the door.

"No, Ethan." Danato knew the look of dismay that Ethan would have even before he turned around. "I need you to go home and sleep."

"What? My wife is—"

"—is safely contained for the time being. I need you rested so you can deal with the Council of the Moon tomorrow..." Danato checked the clock. "Later this morning."

"I won't be able to sleep!"

"You will," Danato insisted. "Just go home. I'll talk to Cori. Belus will get on the taps to the higher-ups." Belus nodded to assure Ethan that he would. "We'll get this all figured out in a matter of hours."

"I need to see her," Ethan said quietly, but with as much force as he could without simply demanding it.

"I know, and I understand the urgency you're feeling, but I'd like to speak with her first." Danato's tone offered the apology for his misuse of authority.

Ethan shook his head. "I just don't understand this. She hates Efrat. Why would she help him? And why would he help her? He's tried to kill her more than once."

Danato nodded. "I'm about to find that out. Please, go update Daniel before he obliterates the house and get some sleep." Ethan mumbled some kind of respectful compliance before leaving, but Danato couldn't hear it.

"Daniel?" Belus probed about the mention of his former protégé.

"He didn't take the general's presence too well last night."

"Did he attack him?" Belus rutted his brow. As much faith as Belus put in Daniel, he knew as well as anyone that the power he possessed didn't mesh well with his temper. It had taken Belus the better part of a year to instruct him on the finer points of anger management. Even Cori's intense schedule couldn't compete with the hours Belus had put into Daniel's rehabilitation.

"No, but I think he came very close. I wouldn't advise letting them meet again. I'm not entirely sure what pissed him off so much. I never thought of him as the heroic type."

Belus nodded in agreement.

"I'd better go talk to Cori." Danato headed for the door.

"Are you sure you should be the one to talk to her?"

Danato paused. He knew Belus was asking in earnest, but he hated that he thought he needed to ask.

"This is beyond the territory of a duty roster, Belus. I am still the warden of this prison."

"I only mean that she didn't come to you with this prior to doing it. She didn't trust you to back her up."

"She didn't come to you either." Danato managed to say it without sounding petty, but it was still a pejorative statement either way.

"I wouldn't expect her to," Belus said. "She knows I won't bend the rules to suit her."

Danato glared back at him.

Belus held up his hands in surrender before he could offer another scathing remark. "I'm not picking a fight, Danato. It just seems to me that since Cori's time-jumping encounter, she's been rather guarded with you. She may be reluctant in her honesty if she thinks it will piss you off. She needs a little compassion."

"Good God, Belus. Are you instructing me on compassion? Do you really think you are a better choice to offer her that?""No, of course not, but I can keep my opinions out of the conversation and get the answers we need. I'm not nearly as emotionally invested in her as you are."

"Aren't you?" Danato asked with unintentional ridicule. The statement stalled Belus's resolve.

"Just tell me that you can get her to tell you everything: the motive, the key, Jill, everything. If she's drawn the wrong conclusions about this, she just let three of the most dangerous entities we house out into the world. I don't care about your feelings, or her ego, just get the information."

Danato wanted to wring his neck for the condescension, but he was right. Cori's insistence on keeping secrets and dealing with problems herself was reinforced by her concern that he would not listen to her or trust her when the time came. If Belus walked up to her and demanded the truth, she would tell him, not because she respected him more, but because she knew he wouldn't judge her. Belus would listen to everything without the emotionally charged reactions Danato usually offered.

Danato remembered thinking that Belus would have to adjust how he treated Cori in order to earn her trust, but it seemed he was now taking a lesson from him. He would have to stop reacting to her like she was a misbehaving child. At the moment, she was a trusted employee who just did something really stupid. He would have to treat her as such.

"I'll get it out of her," he said and left Belus to figure out how to get out of this mess by the book, so Clark didn't cart Cori back to America.

3

CORI SAT ON THE bed of her prison cell with her knees tucked to her chest. It was poetic justice—if poetic justice meant being bitch-slapped by irony. It was the same cell that Vince spent his part-time hours in as a man. The room had no evidence of her deceased lover. She imagined it might still smell like him, but it didn't. It was just a cell. A place she used to visit. Like her memories of him, it was no longer a part of her life. She had once loved him so much, but now she barely thought of him. That seemed so sad to her.

She had spent the remainder of the night in the cell, but she hadn't really slept. She kept waiting for Danato to pop in and slam his hands against the cell door, demanding an explanation. She dreaded it at first, but after she saw the sun peek through the high windows, she began to hope for it.

She hoped someone would come see her. She needed to correct General Clark's version of her actions. She needed them all to understand that Efrat and the others weren't criminals; they were victims. She needed to plateau the antagonism she had created so she could start negotiations on the elementals' behalf.

When she finally heard footsteps in the hall, she jumped up to greet her visitor. She was more than disappointed to see Clark. Even his face, smiling as it was, felt like an instant threat to her life. She wanted to kill him.

She, who had capitulated to help her former murderer out of veneration for life, wanted to close her hands around Clark's throat and watch the life drain from his eyes. She knew it was probably Jill's residual memories that prompted such a strong reaction to him, but she wasn't sure it mattered. In that moment, she wanted him dead, regardless of whose idea it was.

Cori stood at the door, gripping the bars so she didn't reach out and grab his throat. Clark gave her porch lion guards the nod, and they shuffled off to give them privacy. Before they were out of earshot, he spoke loudly enough to be heard. "I hope you slept well, Mrs. Pierce."

"I slept just fine," she lied. "My conscience doesn't keep me awake at night. What about you, General?"

He grimaced. "I haven't had the chance to sleep yet. I've been dealing with the backlash of your meddling." Clark donned a smirk. Much like his smile, it made her want to back away in defense, but her ego refused to offer him the satisfaction of domination. "But to answer your question, I sleep well at night as well."

She opened her mouth to speak, but he moved abruptly to the door and gripped her arms through the bars. The pinch behind her elbows made her wince, but she didn't back away. For the moment, she was in pain, but she was safe behind the bars.

"I'm not usually the type of man that people don't take seriously, Mrs. Pierce."

"Don't worry, it's not personal. I'm not the type of woman to take any authority figure seriously." He pinched harder, and she cringed.

"I thought we had an understanding. What prompted you to go back on our agreement?"

"You shouldn't have threatened their lives. I can't abide watching you kill anyone else."

"Tell me what you know. What did Jill tell you?"

"I know everything," she rasped, trying to pull his elbows away, but his grip had jammed her between him and the bars she was gripping. "I know how you forced Jill to steroid your volunteers until their powers were so strong they couldn't even touch anyone. You destroyed four—five lives because you were in such a damned hurry."

"And yet, Mrs. Pierce, *you* seem to have no trouble touching them." Cori felt her body sweat instantly from the accusation. "Why is that?"

His face was close enough that she could smell the cough drop on his breath. "I'm just special, I guess."

Clark's eyes went cold and his grip on her elbows released enough to offer her blood flow. "Cori." He said her name so quietly that it made her breath hasten with concern. "I saw your rings glowing. I felt what you did to me after that global winter struck. You froze my hands."

"That had nothing to do with me. It was just the globe."

He grinned. "Then why are the bars you're gripping so tightly covered in ice?"

Cori looked down and found her hands and the bars she was hanging onto encased in ice. She panicked, trying to remove her hands, but she was stuck. Clark removed his grasp, since it was no longer necessary. "Interesting," he said, looking her over. "Very interesting."

He didn't level any more threats or ask any questions. He just walked away, happy and content with the answers she had already given him.

4

WITH A LITTLE CONCENTRATION, Cori melted the ice with some of Garr's absorbed power before the guards returned. Almost as soon as they were in position, Danato approached the cell and nodded them off again. They conferred non-verbally, before giving him space to have a semi-private conversation instead of getting their skulls bashed in. Smart men.

"Danato." Cori brought her arms through the bars to offer him the connection that he undoubtedly wanted after watching her being torn away from him, but she couldn't quite reach him. When it was clear that he was keeping the space between them open, she let down her reach and landed her head harshly against the bars. "Danato, I'm so sorry."

"Let's skip all that for now," he said flatly, without the anger or embitterment she'd expected from him. "I need to know what happened."

"General Clark—" she continued from where they had left off at the house.

"Starting with the key you took from my center desk drawer."

Cori's mouth fell open as she realized how far back she needed to take this story to keep him satisfied with her loyalty. He crossed his arms, waiting for her response.

"Danato, I didn't—" she started, but he interrupted, assuming that she was going to deny the accusation—which she was, but only partially.

"The key, Cori," he said as if she was a simpleton. The derision was more than a little painful. "When did you find it? When did you open my drawer?" He paused to swallow. "What did you read?"

Cori nodded and held up a surrendering hand before she spoke. She considered telling him she just found the key, like he assumed, but she was certain the truth would only come back to haunt her if she didn't admit it here and now. "I wasn't the one who found the key. I never even paid attention to the locked drawer. I got the key from Efrat." She could see his eyes narrow just at the mention of that name. She was a long way from convincing him to offer asylum. "He slipped it into my mouth when he kissed me." She bit back her lips, hoping to shunt away the memory of his lips on hers.

"Why didn't you tell me about it?" She could tell he was trying to keep his emotions out of the conversation, but she could still hear a hint of accusation in his tone.

"Efrat... it doesn't matter what he said. He made me doubt your intentions regarding their containment."

His jaw shifted like he wanted to speak, but he didn't. She appreciated his restraint, but she felt more nervous waiting for his explosion than just getting it out of the way.

"I didn't believe him, Danato. He was just another ex-con claiming innocence."

"But you kept the key."

"Yes, I kept the key." She paused, trying to remember the thought process that led to that conclusion. "I was upset, confused, blah, blah, blah... I wanted the truth. I didn't think you would give it to me. So much of you is still hidden from me."

His eyes danced over her like he wanted to respond to that. "You broke into my office to read the elemental files?"

"I wasn't aware that your office was off limits to me." As soon as she said it, his eyes blazed. She lowered her gaze, trying to make up for her derision. "Yes, I did."

"When?"

She took in a breath and looked down. "I..."

"When?" His face went dark and his eyes narrowed.

"I slipped out during the party." She braced herself for his volume, but it didn't come.

"You slipped out during the party." His voice was soft and laden with disbelief. "The party I put on as a present for you? You chose that particular occasion to spy on me?"

"Danato..."

"Did you plan this with Efrat? Have you been planning this with Efrat?"

"No, nothing... Aside from the inconvenient timing of my curiosity, nothing was planned about last night. I had every intention of saying my goodbyes and coming straight home."

"What changed, Cori?" Danato's volume was more scolding than angry, but she was relieved that he had not gone completely stony on her. "That's the question that has me, Ethan, and Belus pondering in circles. What the fuck happened between you dressed in crimson, dancing the night away, and you spattered in crimson, releasing the most dangerous prisoners in this facility?"

"They are not the danger in this," Cori pleaded, hoping to get a start on her negotiations.

"They *are*!" Danato bellowed. "They've been here for six years. They've killed a dozen of my men in that time."

Cori cringed at his volume as she always did, but she refused to let this meeting be about him telling her his estimations of the elementals. She already knew how he felt about them, but he didn't know as much as she did. "Jillian Frank knew them before they had powers. They weren't born with these abilities. They were a human-weapons project gone wrong. Clark put them all here to hide them. They weren't viable for field use, and I doubt any of them would have helped him after the hell they were put through to get their so-called superpowers."

"How the fuck do you know all this?"

"I know they killed your people, but they were trying to escape." Cori paused, wondering if that was accurate to say, since Efrat had suggested it was impossible. "Or maybe they just stopped caring about living and dying. At any rate, Efrat never saw any difference between the monster holding him captive and the monster renting the room out to him so he could do it. He was just fighting whomever was keeping him contained."

Danato shook his head and shrugged, trying to assimilate her words and find his own. "Why didn't you come to me with this information the minute Jill told you?"

Cori flinched at her lie of omission, but pushed onward. Her growing issues with her rings could be dealt with later. Danato already had enough reasons to be mad at her. "After I found out who Jill was, I followed her upstairs. I wasn't able to stop her from killing the two guards, but I stopped her from killing Hirem. I was about to talk her out of her irrational decision when—"

Cori gulped back her volume before continuing to speak, but she still spat the words out with the same disgust she'd felt at the time. "Clark shot her. She was inches from my face when the back of her head exploded." Cori threw out her hand to describe the distance a little more thoroughly. "I didn't know what to do! I wanted to strangle Clark with my bare hands, but I just yelled at him. Then Hirem picked up the gun and went after Clark."

"He attacked Clark with a gun," Danato said flatly, like an investigator taking down the notes from a witness.

Cori frowned. "I don't think he really intended to shoot him. I think he just wanted to die with a clean soul."

Danato wavered at her insight into Hirem, but he urged her to go on.

"I was angry and sad. I can't explain all that now, but just believe me that I felt personally affected by watching them die. After he shot Hirem, I went after Clark. I suppose to strangle him like I wanted to." Cori glanced down at her hands. "I don't know. Efrat stopped me. He made me listen to reason. He knew what Clark was. He knew how much danger I was in. He told me to leave and not come back."

"You left." Danato's eyes narrowed. "You didn't just break them out then."

"I was on my way out the door when Clark caught me. He talked about having that meeting with you."

"Yes, I understood that part."

"No, you don't, because Clark wasn't offering a meeting so we could discuss what happened. He was offering a chance for me to keep my mouth shut so he could describe the events in his own words. He expected me to back him up." Cori could see this didn't surprise Danato. She wasn't being blunt enough. "Danato, he was going to kill me."

His eyes widened like she hoped they would.

"I don't mean he was angry enough to kill me. I mean, he had the gun pulled, and he was seeing if I would cooperate to cover up the mess, or if he would have to kill me. The line was drawn and I barely kiss-assed my way over it.

"After he was done threatening my life, he threatened Efrat and the others. He put their lives in my hands. I know you're mad, Danato, but I was going to wind up walking in with a lie either way last night. Either my lie or his, and I chose mine."

"Then what happened?"

"I left."

Danato stepped forward and leaned on her door. He wasn't offering affection, so she didn't reach out to him. "Explain to me why you didn't pick up that phone right then and call me."

"I didn't think you would help the way I wanted you to."

"You didn't think I would help let them go? You're damn right I wouldn't." He glared at her through the bars.

"No, I didn't think you would help them at all. I've read the files, Danato. They have no convictions. Hell, they don't even have any charges against them. You signed the paperwork to put four people in this prison and hold them indefinitely when the only crime they committed was not cooperating with a militaristic government."

"That's what you got out of reading those files? You think I housed them for the money?"

"What other interpretation is there?"

Danato moved away, taking a moment to think before he responded. "Invasion of privacy aside, did you happen to see another file in that drawer?"

Cori thought back to that night. "There was one other file marked *Deceased* in red?" she offered, more as a question than a statement.

"I take it you didn't read it."

"No, I wasn't interested in lingering," she murmured.

"Did you wonder why it was in there?"

Cori sighed, not understanding why he was dragging out his point. "No, I was preoccupied. Why are you even bringing it up?"

"You said there was no other way to interpret why I would sign off on the elementals when their histories were clean." Danato turned to her. "I am offering you another interpretation so that your flagrant mistrust for me can be alleviated." He spoke softly, but the disdain was still there. "The deceased prisoner file was my wife's."

Cori was already looking at him, so she couldn't afford more shock than her mouth dropping open and her eyes bulging. She couldn't remember the first conversation they'd ever had about his wife. She couldn't remember if he had mentioned she had been a prisoner.

At the same time, she realized how close she was to getting answers about the part of Danato's past that he refused to share. She respected his privacy enough not to pester him about it, but she wasn't sure she would have passed up the file if she had understood what it was.

"Did you check the dates by the signatures in the elemental files?"

Cori shook her head. She could already see where this was going and her heart ached to think of it.

"It's the same date as on that deceased stamp on the front of her file. I signed those papers the same day I signed my wife's death certificate."

She frowned at him as he approached the bars. She reached her hands out to him, but he bypassed her and reached through the bars to grab her under the chin.

She instinctively pressed on his chest, prepared to push him away. He noted the movement and caressed her cheek with his thumb like that had been his intention all along. "Now, as someone familiar with the loss of a lover, you tell me: do you think I read those fucking files?"

Danato's voice reached a new depth, and his grip tightened on her face. She shook her head as best she could. Tears of empathy and shame poured down into his hand. "If you had brought me the key and expressed your concerns about his incarceration, I would have read through the file. I would have seen the misdirection. We could have fixed this, Cori! Together!"

He dropped his hand, taking in a breath as he looked her over with the same disappointment she had seen in him so many times. "You are so worried about whether you can trust me, but you never give me a reason to trust you." Danato gripped the door. "If you ever go behind my back like this again, I will suspend you. You will be back on cleaning duty like your first fucking day! Do you understand?"

Cori's heart clenched. She had never considered being demoted so low. The thought of going back to janitorial work made this entire place seem intolerable. "Yes, sir." Her voice shook. Her subservient prescribed response only amplified her disaffection.

His expression softened, but only enough to make her hope that he would offer reassurance of his love, which he didn't. "Why didn't you tell me about it all before Clark came to get you?"

"In case you didn't agree to not send the collectors out right away. I knew they would need time to get away." Cori could feel the lie roll off her tongue and she hated it, but it was too soon to ask Danato for asylum. She needed to let this moment play out. When he was calm again, she could negotiate with him. "And... I just didn't want to. I knew this would be the end result either way." She motioned to her cell. "I just wanted another hour of normalcy before all my screw-ups caught up with me." Her tears trickled down. She didn't bother wiping them away. "I just wanted another hour before I lost every last ounce of your trust."

If the conviction in her voice remotely affected Danato, he didn't show it. "Cori," he said firmly, "I may still need to send the collectors out after them. I can't just let them run free. They may not have to go back to Clark, but we will have to register them and decide what to do with them. Especially if they are haphazardly or accidentally going to burn, drench, and electrocute things. Do you understand that?"

"Does that mean you might be able to offer them asylum?" Her voice pitched a little too much, revealing her enthusiasm.

"I don't know. I can't answer that yet. That will be for Belus to figure out with our head bureaucrats. You've dug us in too deep to do this under the table. We have to go by the books now, or risk being audited. Believe me, as much as you hate being under my thumb, you would despise an audit."

Cori exhaled, feeling the stress of now having to convince Belus that the elementals should be taken from Clark. Oh, the joy of paperwork. She hated doing things by the book. She hated books. Reading—words—snore. "When do you think I can get out of here?"

"If I give him the elementals back, Clark will release you of his own free will. Supposedly," Danato added as an afterthought.

"You think he might try to detain me?"

Danato shrugged. "It's nothing. I just don't trust him."

"Neither do I." She grimaced. "I should have just let Daniel kill him," she murmured.

Danato reached his hand through the bars and caressed her cheek. She leaned into his hand like it was a life preserver to her drowning body. "You leave Clark to me, Cori. If anyone is going to be aiming weapons or fists at him, it will be me. Understood?"

She nodded into his hand. As he pulled it away, she clasped onto it with both hands. "Danato!" He paused to listen to her. "You'll forgive me eventually, won't you? You'll always forgive me, won't you?"

He pulled his hand out despite her vehement grip on him. He took in a deep breath, letting his exhaustion show as he exhaled. "Yes, Cori, I will always forgive you... eventually." He walked away, not allowing her a retort. She wondered how much more he was going to hate her when he found out that the elementals hadn't even escaped.

5

Daniel hadn't intended to fall asleep on the couch. When he heard the door shut, he snapped upright. Ethan stood at the door, looking every bit as pissed as when he'd left. Heaton got up from the chair he had been napping in and met him at the door. "How did it go?" he asked.

"Procedure bullshit." Ethan ripped off his coat and hung it up. "We have to check with the board before proceeding."

"Feck that, just go break her out," Daniel contributed, hanging over the back of the couch. Heaton gave him a look that said he wasn't helping matters.

"I haven't even talked to her yet. Danato wants to talk with her first."

"Feck that, she's your wife," Daniel spouted again.

"Dude!" Heaton scolded, since he didn't get the hint with the scowl. "I'm sure this will all pass. She's not in any danger. Danato just has to figure out how to proceed, so he doesn't make things worse." Heaton looked back at Daniel. "That's how things work in the grown-up world."

"What?" Daniel shrugged innocently.

"What about the grown-up world?" Nevia asked as she strolled downstairs, yawning. She was still in her pajamas, rightfully so, since the sun was barely up. She was wearing the loose-fitting t-shirt that she had worn her first night with Daniel. He cringed at seeing the memorabilia, but only because he liked it so much.

"Where the hell have you been, bloodhound? You missed everything," he rebuked.

She looked at them all. "I was sleeping. I couldn't hear anything. What happened?"

"Serves you right, going to bed early. I'll tell you what happened," Daniel began.

"Daniel," Heaton interrupted. "Do some breathing exercises or something before you lob off someone's head with a glare." He made it sound like a jibe since they were in company, but he gave him a stern look that suggested he needed to be careful.

Daniel generally kept his temper in check, for obvious reasons, but something about the intrusion into the house last night had set him off. He wasn't sure if it was the attack on Cori or simply the disruption of what should have been a nice evening, or because he had just had a blow-out with Nevia and he was already on edge. No matter the reason, he needed to calm down.

"Fine, you tell her. I'm going to make coffee." Daniel jumped up and headed to the kitchen. On the way by, Ethan mumbled something to Heaton about filling her in so he could rest. Daniel exchanged a glance with Heaton as Ethan jaunted upstairs.

While he filled the water pitcher for coffee, he took in some deep breaths. It probably looked as asinine as it felt, but it made him feel a little better. Nevia settled on a stool at the end of the island, while Heaton joined him in the kitchen.

Heaton reached over his shoulder for the basket of tea bags. Daniel waved him away. "I got it."

"You don't know how I like it."

Daniel turned to him. "Earl Grey, dash of cream, no sugar. I know your bleeding drink, you eejit. Just because I don't wake up on the edge of your bed in the morning doesn't mean I can't make a fecking cup of tea."

Heaton looked almost suspicious of the offer. "You don't usually offer."

"Cause I'm not a poof, but I'm making coffee for Miss Late Start, so I'm already outdoing my gentlemanly hospitality for the year."

Heaton looked at Nevia. She shook her head in response to a question he didn't actually ask.

"Alright, back to it," Heaton said and settled down on the stool next to Nevia to explain last night's events, leading up to the all-nighter for Ethan. By the time the coffee had percolated and the tea had steeped, Nevia was up to speed.

"Damn it, the only good gunfight I'll ever see in this place and I missed it," Nevia said without the humor that a less gun-crazy woman might have. "Sorry guys, didn't mean to drop the ball."

"There was no ball, just the usual juggling act that comes with this place." Daniel slid her coffee over pre-doctored. "Taste it." He gave Heaton his and waited for him to taste as well.

"Well, I'll be damned. The man can make a cup of tea," Heaton said after tasting his tea.

Daniel perked an eyebrow and waited for Nevia to taste hers. She nodded. "Perfect, that's impressive. Usually people put too much sugar in and not enough cream."

"See, I can do more than drink and get laid."

Heaton scoffed. "Barely."

Daniel smiled at his taunt, but when he saw Nevia's sober reaction, he lost it. He sipped on his own coffee, which needed no special attention like his partner's. "No beer last night and tea service this morning. What bug got into your bonnet?"

"A really bitchy one," he mumbled into his cup before taking another sip.

Heaton glanced between them. "Did I miss something?"

Daniel cleared his throat and put down his coffee. He was willing to do just about anything to change the subject. "Do you want me to fix your arm?" Heaton instinctively reached to check if his sleeve was covering his scar. "I can now, if you want. I understand if you're uncomfortable with me doing anything more to you."

Heaton looked at Nevia. She nodded. "He can. I've been helping him develop his reversal power. He's reluctant to do it because he's afraid of hurting anyone, but he's capable of healing you. You'll be as smooth as the day you were born."

"I'm thinking about opening a salon to do facial reconstruction for wrinkled old birds."

"Daniel," Nevia quietly scolded. He could tell she didn't like it when he mocked his own ability. He wasn't sure why. Whether she admitted it, that was a viable use for his skills.

"Anyway, I just figured I'd offer."

Heaton looked down at his arm. The shirt was still covering it, but he didn't need to remove it to see the damage. It had been there long enough to memorize it. "Does it hurt?" he asked with trepidation.

"A little at first," Nevia answered for Daniel. Heaton didn't really agree to anything one way or another, but Nevia slipped off her stool and took his hand. "Come on."

Heaton seemed a little resistant, but in the end he followed her like a man being dragged to the gallows. It was an odd scene to witness Nevia dragging a reluctant man upstairs to her bedroom. Why would any man be reluctant to follow her to her bedroom? It could very well be to his death, and Daniel would still follow her willingly.

Daniel grabbed the ice packs from the freezer, along with a few frozen veggies. He didn't really want to do this again, but he owed Heaton for scarring him in the first place. He also wanted to exert some choice over his power, not to mention prove that he wasn't a complete arse. He was probably mostly an arse, but not completely.

Nevia's bedroom was much like his own, but with a few more feminine touches. The house always amazed him with how quickly it reflected its guests' personalities. If he had ever taken the time to think about it further, he might have found it creepy. A living house was just a bit over his threshold of comfort, so he just didn't think about it—a solution that he found worked in many areas of his life.

He usually took this same approach with women, but Nevia was different. Last night, he had meant every word he said to her. He wanted nothing more to do with her. This morning, however, was another story. This morning, he was back at square one. He wanted to be that guy she thought he was. He wasn't exactly sure if he could do it, but he could at least try.

"What's with the ice packs?" Heaton asked as Daniel tossed them on the bedside table.

"The reversal of his power causes..." Nevia started to explain as she pulled her comforter up over her pillows. She caught Daniel looking at her and she naturally interpreted his annoyance to be from her speaking on his behalf. However, his irritation stemmed more from the peep show he got when she leaned over the bed. No one likes to smell freshly baked bread when they can't eat it. And yet, they continue to make candles scented like food.

"Sorry," she apologized for her conversational dominance. "Did you want to explain?" He mumbled a retraction and motioned for her to continue. "The healing power..." she continued while Daniel sat down on the edge of the bed. It was probably the closest he would ever get to being in her bed. "...reverses the thermal reaction in him. Instead of getting dangerously cold with a low heart rate, he gets dangerously hot with a high heart rate." Daniel resisted the urge to make a joke about being hot.

"Dangerously hot. Didn't you put that on your resume?" Heaton offered a joke up for him. Daniel chuckled at it. He was happy that things were back to some semblance of camaraderie between them. He still didn't understand why Heaton could trust Nevia with his secret and not him, but he couldn't balk at it too much if Heaton was in a better mood because of it.

"Yeah, right before *plays well with others*," Daniel added. "Okay, get over here before my peas melt." He patted the bed.

Heaton coughed. "Seriously, we have to do this on a bed?"

Daniel looked back at Nevia, who was kneeling on the mattress behind him.

"Come on, like it isn't a dream come true for you," Daniel chided. Heaton rolled his eyes. "Get on with it. I promise I won't touch your gooter."

"He's a pain in the ass to lift, so I prefer if he passes out on the bed," Nevia offered a more rational explanation.

Heaton joined them on the bed, lying between them. He smiled after he got into position, like the image of Nevia crouched on one side and Daniel sitting on the other had taken the joke to a whole new level.

Daniel wanted to make another joke, but it only would have been to stall. He grabbed Heaton's forearm and turned it over. He looked back up at him. Heaton was nervous, and he looked a little angry, but he didn't object to anything.

Daniel could see Nevia watching him out of the corner of his eye as he focused his energy. She was such a contradiction in his life. People always avoided looking at him. Sometimes they didn't even know why, they just instinctively pulled away. Conversely, she was drawn to him. Not in the way that he preferred, but...

He wasn't used to that kind of attention. He certainly wasn't used to the admiration of his power. It made him uncomfortable. She was right to push him, though. If he was going to wield a power great enough to destroy a being, he should at least learn how to undo some of the damage he created.

Unfortunately, *that* realization meant he would have to apologize to her—which he planned to do after he woke up.

6

DANIEL WOKE TO THE sound of Heaton and Nevia talking about his recovered arm. He didn't need to hear the words to know that Heaton was pleased. His arm was back to new and probably without so much as a freckle. He really could blow the beauty industry out of the water.

"How did it go?" Daniel asked, more to announce his consciousness than to get an update.

"Dude." Heaton stepped over and showed him his arm. "This is amazing."

Daniel rolled to his side to see the pubescent skin on his arm. "It's all for you, buddy." Daniel intended it as a joke, but in a way Heaton was on his list of reasons to continue with Nevia's intrigue despite not getting sex out of it. "I'm sorry I put you through it to begin with."

Heaton must have sensed the somber tone in his voice, because he slapped him on the shoulder. "Don't worry about it. How's the heart?" He pressed his finger to his throat. "That's still pretty high. Are you sure he'll be okay?"

"Yeah." Nevia leaned in behind Heaton to check his temperature with the back of her hand pressed to his forehead. He vaguely remembered her tossing her ear thermometer on his bed. She hadn't expected to need it again. "He's actually not being affected as much as he was originally."

"How would you know?" Daniel asked with a little more offense than he intended.

"Because you're awake," she reproved right back.

Heaton turned, and they spoke as if he were a patient, completely unnecessary to the diagnosing process. "I think as he develops this power he will be affected less and less. At some point, I imagine, he could actually do it without passing out, though he might still have the spike in temperature and heart rate."

"Like developing cardio stamina," Heaton suggested.

"Precisely," she agreed.

"Why does he still risk dying when he uses his destructive power?" Heaton asked, as if she had suddenly become the foremost expert on dispersers.

"I suspect it has something to do with the energy expenditure. The heart and lungs can develop stamina for cardio exercise. The destructive power is more like weightlifting—he can do it, but he will be sore afterwards, and he has to rebuild the muscle tissue before he can do it again."

"But he doesn't necessarily get bigger muscles to do it better."

She waved her hand like the analogy got fuzzy at that point. "I suspect that when he removes a transmorph from a human, he could utilize both powers at the same time, and therefore balance his reaction to it."

"Really?" Heaton asked with gasping interest.

"Really?" Daniel asked with far less audible enthusiasm.

"Yes," she looked at Daniel with disappointment quickly creeping into her eyes, "but that's neither here nor there, since Daniel isn't interested in continuing this." Nevia moved off to her duffel bag and found a set of clean clothes for the day. Without regard for either of them, she turned her back to them and exchanged her t-shirt for a button-down shirt. Daniel looked at her large serpentine tattoo like a fond memory.

Heaton looked back at him for an answer. "You aren't going to keep developing your power?"

Daniel shrugged. "I don't know," he said honestly. It wasn't quite an admission of defeat to her badgering, but she paused to hear what else he had to say. "I'm not sure I can live up to what Nevia has in mind. She thinks I'm a new messiah."

"I do not think that." She turned back and gave him a stern glare that told him he had caught a nerve, or just offended her with his blasphemy. "I just..."

A wall-shaking knock on her door interrupted Nevia. "Nevia, Heaton, anyone," Danato's voice thundered despite the thick door.

"Shit, it's Danato," Daniel said, forcing himself to sit up. He pushed the ice packs and vegetables under the covers and tried to look casual, even though he was still panting and sweating. There was really no reason to hide anything from Danato, but Daniel had learned long ago that his particular personality put the big man into a rage pretty quick. Just stealing his frozen vegetables might be enough to set him off.

Nevia quickly slipped on her fresh pants and zipped herself on the way to the door. She opened it and Danato stepped in just enough to ensure that the door couldn't be closed on him prematurely. He gazed over the room, taking in Daniel panting on the bed, Heaton standing near him, and Nevia by the door, not quite back to her all-business self yet.

"What's going on here?" he asked. Daniel could tell Danato was trying to put it all together on his own. If they had been missing clothing, he might have assumed something despicable, but since Daniel was the only one out of breath and everyone was clothed, it was throwing off the logic of any conclusion he was trying to reach.

"We were just discussing our game plan." Nevia said the lie as diplomatically as she would the truth. "We planned on leaving today, but with Cori in trouble again, we weren't sure we should."

Danato eyed Daniel one last time before turning his attention to Nevia. "Yes, I was just coming to speak with you about that. Belus and I are going to be busy trying to get things under control. I may need Ethan to keep things operational. Unfortunately, the Council of the Moon is not willing to postpone their trial. Actually, I didn't even ask them." He lifted his hands, half in surrender, half in a shrug. They all understood what fem-wolves were like. "Anyway, I was wondering if you guys could keep an eye on the proceedings for us."

"Of course we will," Nevia said.

"Hey, don't volunteer us," Daniel griped.

"Of course we will," Heaton said, a little firmer.

"Apparently we will." Daniel frowned.

"Good." Danato stared at him. "Daniel, may I speak to you alone?"

Daniel was not exactly a spring chicken—his twenties were a distant memory, and his forties were an ever-looming future for him—but when Danato said those words, he felt twelve years old again.

7

THERE WASN'T ACTUALLY A decision made on whether Daniel was open to a discussion. Danato just left the room with the implied expectation that he should follow him. Heaton gave him a smile that told him he felt bad for him, but it wouldn't stop him from being amused by it. As Daniel walked past him, Heaton patted him on the back.

Daniel turned to him and grabbed his shoulders. He spoke with mock seriousness. "If I don't come back, I just want you to know... I've always hated your hair."

Heaton snorted and rolled his eyes while he pushed Daniel on to continue his walk of shame. He thought about grabbing Nevia and giving her a real mock goodbye kiss, but the humor would be lost on her, and knowing his luck, she would actually get pissed off about it. Instead, he lowered his head like a frightened dog and headed to his verbal beating.

Danato stood behind the couch, waiting for Daniel to join him. Since he hadn't positioned himself in his chair, Daniel already knew this wouldn't be a pleasant talk. He chuckled at the thought of what was to come and took a seat on a stool at the end of the island. It left an uncomfortable conversational distance, but an ass-ripping didn't exactly count as comfortable to begin with.

"What's on your mind, Danato?" Daniel asked, sensing the silence that he was using to set the mood. He did it for intimidation, but to Daniel it was just irksome.

"Last night," Danato crossed his arms, "you seemed to have a little trouble backing down."

Daniel smiled. "Yeah, I was a little threatened by the military coup in the house."

"I want you to know that I appreciate the ferocity with which you defend your friends."

Daniel nodded and pinched his lips to rein in his smile. This was only Danato's diplomacy at work. He started with the compliment to balance out the reprimand. Unfortunately, one civil comment from Danato was not enough to balance out his tyrannical attitude. "But?" Daniel added to speed things along. Danato gave a hint of a smirk before continuing.

"But I need to know if you have control of yourself or not. I can't have you flying off the handle just because a situation arises that's going to be difficult to resolve."

"Just so we're clear..." Daniel raised a finger. "You're criticizing me for my bad temper. That's kind of like sending the wind to put out a forest fire, isn't it?"

Danato's eyes narrowed. Daniel knew it wasn't a wise statement, but he didn't care. He wasn't one of Danato's prized apprentices. He wasn't going to just roll over and beg for his approval. Technically, he wasn't even an employee, so he wouldn't suck up to him either.

"When I get angry, the only thing in danger is walls and furniture. When you get angry, lives could be lost."

"That's bullocks and you know it. You're like a damn Hercules with that dragon wank juice."

"My temperament is under control. Yours..."

"...is under control. You want to know my status, ask Heaton."

"I have, and now I'm asking you." Danato stepped forward. "Don't think for one second that you are free from this place, Daniel; one screw-up and you're back in prison."

"Like I don't know that," Daniel sneered. "I see it written on your face every time you look at me." Daniel waved his hand over his face. "I don't know what I did to piss you off so much, but whatever it was, it certainly wasn't meant to be personal, so why don't you cut me some slack?"

"You're a murderer, Daniel." Danato mentioned the word like it was an occupation for him. "You don't deserve breaks."

Daniel couldn't find any words to defend himself. He couldn't even find a valid insult. He agreed with Danato. There wasn't any room for defense.

"So, I'll ask you again: with the safety of your partners in mind, do I need to be concerned about your anger management?"

Daniel wasn't sure what to say. His head was drooping again. He wanted to say that there was no reason for him to be concerned, but he wondered. Last night had been intense.

If he had truly gotten out of control...

If he had used his powers...

"May I interject?" Nevia descended the stairs with Heaton behind her.

Danato bristled at the interruption. "This doesn't concern you two."

"Apparently it does," Nevia said, moving right into Danato's path of condemnation. Daniel mentally kicked himself for not warning her about him. She was about to find out for herself. He glanced at Heaton to give him a glare for letting her interrupt, but his eyes were fixated on the face-off emerging between the petite gun-happy Nevia and the ill-tempered ogre Danato.

"You mentioned us as the consideration for his answer. If that's the case, then we should have a chance to weigh in on the topic. After all, we are the ones who work with him. It is our lives on the line."

It impressed Daniel that Danato had let her get as far as she had. It was probably out of his reluctance to shout at women, or perhaps he just assumed that if he brandished his volume at her, she might wilt and cry. Perhaps Danato had a few things to learn as well.

"I've already read Heaton's reports."

"And you don't believe him?" Nevia asked.

"He has gotten close to Daniel over the years. I would hate for his judgment to be swayed by their friendship." Danato looked at Heaton. "I heard about your little mishap. That didn't exactly make it into your reports."

"What mishap?" Nevia said, drawing his attention again. "The incident in which Heaton's ignorance of the gravity of Daniel's power caused him to be foolhardy enough to get in the way of a disperser?" Danato flinched slightly at the label, but didn't interrupt to ask about the designation. Heaton lowered his eyes at Nevia's harsh interpretation of the accident. "The consequences were severe, but the lesson was learned."

"He could have killed him!" Danato tried to interpose, but Nevia didn't actually stop speaking.

"Just as the consequences are severe for mistakes made inside of that prison. We have one supernatural force to be concerned with. This prison houses hundreds."

"And they are all locked up. He isn't."

"No, nor should he be. He is a valuable member of this team. Without him, transmorph hosts cannot be saved." Danato opened his mouth to speak, but he didn't actually say anything. Daniel could sense something strange that he had never seen in his demeanor. Could it be? Danato Calibria was speechless? "The incident you referred to involving Heaton has been repaired."

Nevia motioned for Heaton to come forward. Heaton did so and pulled up his sleeves to show two perfect arms, one slightly more perfect than the other. Danato eyed the flesh with increasing befuddlement.

"You asked Daniel if his temper is under control," Nevia continued. "You don't believe Heaton and his progress reports. I doubt you would believe Daniel's self-analysis. So, believe me when I say, in the last few months working with Daniel, his temper hasn't risen above great irritation or defense of his heart. It has certainly never reached the peak that you are at right now."

Danato furrowed his brow. He may have been told about her abilities, but no one really got it until she used it against them. Even he kept forgetting how truly intuitive she was. "If you wish to question *my* ability to read Daniel and properly assess his volatility, then I'll be happy to offer you a demonstration by telling you how you got your limp."

Danato's shoulders pulled back and his chest puffed up. Daniel stood from his stool slowly, preparing to pull Nevia away at the first sign of any physical rage from Danato. The irony of that would not have been lost on him. Heaton went so far as to clutch the back of her arm, but she didn't move. Not one inch.

Danato's eyes flickered over hers. Daniel couldn't see her eyes, but he imagined as stubborn as she was, she would be giving him a sort of "just try me" look. He wasn't sure what she had sensed about the leg injury, nor did he know why Danato was at such odds with her knowing it, but his jaw was about to break his teeth.

"I'm more than happy to assist you while I am here," Nevia said, breaking the long silence Danato was demanding, "but any concerns about members of my team should be taken through the proper channels."

"I *am* the proper channels!" Danato blustered.

"You are not in any condition to be deciding the fate of a man's life!" Nevia yelled back. If the situation had not been so dire, Daniel would have laughed. "You are angry at Cori and instead of letting that anger stay with her, you are taking it out on Daniel. He is doing his best to move on from his past, and you are not helping him by exacerbating his shame and self-deprecation."

Danato's shoulders relaxed a little, and he looked at Daniel for the first time since Nevia had interrupted. It was almost as if he was looking for those emotions to be labeled on his clothes.

"Daniel's ability to destroy is only beginning to be countered by his ability to heal. He has the potential to do great things, and I will do whatever it takes to make sure he has a chance to live up to that potential."

Danato looked back at Nevia. The change in his tense body was reflected in hers. For a moment, they stared at each other, letting the battle die down naturally, without words.

At long last, he bowed his head for a moment before speaking at normal volume. "You're right. I'm sorry."

Daniel nearly fell over from shock.

"Daniel, I owe you an apology." At that statement, he actually reached out for the chair at the end of the dining room table. "You and I met under hard circumstances and because of that, I've never quite warmed to your... personality. As usual, I'm dealing with more than my fair share of trouble, but that's no excuse to let my preconceived opinions cloud my judgment. If Heaton and Jordan are willing to vouch for your efforts in rehabilitation, then that should be good enough for me."

Daniel nodded. "Thank you... sir," he said with more respect than he had ever before.

Danato looked Nevia over again. Daniel still couldn't see her face, but he knew what her stoic façade looked like. "I think you'll be able to handle the fem-wolves just fine." With that said, he left the house.

"Well, I'll be damned," Heaton said. "I thought for sure he was going to blow a gasket when you mentioned his leg."

Daniel moved to Nevia and hugged her, lifting her off the ground. She instinctively wrapped her arms around him, but he could tell she didn't like that he was manhandling her. Most men might have been offended by a woman fighting their battles for them, but Nevia had done in a few minutes what he couldn't do in six years—tame the beast.

"Put me down, Daniel," she said with even-toned annoyance, but he didn't.

"Thanks man," he said to Heaton over Nevia's shoulder. "I'm glad you still have my back."

Heaton put out his hand to shake on it. "I always had your back."

Daniel let Nevia slide down from the hug so he could shake Heaton's hand, but he kept his free hand around her back, not quite wanting to let go of her yet. "Are you sure?" Daniel asked, gripping his friend's hand a little tighter than needed for a handshake.

Heaton caught his meaning and nodded. "Yeah, I am." Heaton gave him a slap on the shoulder before pulling away and heading to the door. "Better get going. Those bitches aren't going to wait forever, or at all," he said on the way.

With Heaton's back turned to them, Daniel took a chance he would not normally consider. Nevia was already pulling away, but he pulled her back by her shirt. With her head braced in one hand, and her chin tugged upward by his other, he gave her a quick kiss that was not nearly as wet as he would have liked.

He let her go just as fast as he grabbed her and walked away before he could see the resulting look. It likely would have been shock, but if it was anger, he didn't need to see it, and if it was attraction, he *definitely* didn't need to see it.

8

W HEN ETHAN FINALLY AWOKE an hour past his intended time, a quick phone call to Danato got him up to speed on Cori and the change in delegations of duty. He had intended to observe the trial and possibly even vouch for Callin, but he had more important issues at hand.

Arriving at Cori's cage, he saw her head down and knees tucked to her chest. When she looked up at him through the bars of the door, her face melted instantly to tears. He knew she was feeling guilty for not telling him about the key. The note she had left behind told him she was particularly grieved to put him in a position to worry about her again. He also knew she had been through the wringer with Danato already.

Disgusted by the bars that were separating them, he reached for his keys. The guards flanking her cell put their hands in his way. He didn't even look at them. "She's my wife!" His voluminous voice echoed around the cavernous room. The men exchanged looks and removed the barrier of their hands.

He slid back the door and entered the cell. He closed it behind him, even though the closure offered no particular privacy. Cori buried her head again and shook it. She must have assumed he was as mad as Danato. If he had been thinking about all the details, he might have been, but all he was interested in was getting her out of this mess.

He sat down beside her on the cot and scooped her up, placing her on his lap. She uncurled enough to wrap herself around him and bawl into his shoulder. After a few moments of hiccupping tears, she whispered apologies into his ear. He rubbed her back, but said nothing in response to those apologies. Yet.

There was always time to hold her accountable for the details, but there wasn't always time to hold her.

9

D ANIEL COULDN'T HAVE BEEN more bored. In the back hall of the part-time level, not far from where Cori was being held, aluminum bleachers had been set up for the Council of the Moon and observers to watch the trial.

Daniel and Heaton sat in a side section of bleachers. The nosebleed section was only a couple of meters off the ground, but the back railing offered them the freedom to slouch back. Nevia sat a row below, although there was plenty of room between them.

The council of bitches was in the center set of bleachers, watching the proceedings intently. They all offered Nevia glares as she walked by to get situated, but Heaton and Daniel had gotten a few smiles. It was about as complimentary as a man smiling at his steak, but he couldn't help but enjoy the view as he passed, even if he would never partake.

He may have been a lascivious bastard, but he wasn't stupid. Men who hooked up with fem-wolves had to be comfortable with positions of submission in and out of the bedroom. He didn't mind the submission in the bedroom, but he wasn't about to take a lover that could snap his neck if he didn't compliment her new haircut.

Daniel noticed throughout the trial that one woman in particular was watching Nevia. He didn't like it, but he wasn't sure what to do about it. Nevia either didn't sense it or didn't care, but he kept a watchful eye on the woman, anyway.

From what he gathered from the proceedings, the prisoner named Callin, who was currently in human form, in his human confinement, was pleading for joint custody of his child. The mother was easy to pinpoint by the screaming infant draped over her shoulder and the fussy baby she kept trying to shush by rocking a car seat with her foot. She might have normally been a stylish French woman, but by the looks of the recent additions to her life, self-dedication had gone out the window for her... *and how*.

Callin finished his plea to the council to let him participate in his son Lynnius's rearing and development. The man was young, not much older than Ethan, he thought, but he was mature and well-spoken. His supplication proved his knowledge of his son and genuinely implied his love and devotion to not only him, but to the child's mother.

Daniel nudged Nevia with his foot and she looked back at him. He motioned for her to come up so he could talk to her. She seemed annoyed by the request, but she pushed herself back onto the bench between him and

Heaton. Both Daniel and Heaton leaned forward so the three-way conversation could be done in a whisper.

"So, what's the deal?" Daniel asked. "Is this guy on the level?"

"He has an affection for her and the child, if that's what you mean," she answered, still watching the room even though they were only discussing who would like to question Callin. "He's truthful in his plea."

"They should be able to sense that too," Daniel offered. He wasn't sure why, but he was kind of rooting for the guy. He wasn't a father himself, at least so far as he knew, but he did like children, and being denied the rights to something you helped create just seemed wrong on so many levels.

"It doesn't matter," Heaton said, bursting his still-forming bubble of hope. "The council will never allow a male to raise a child."

"Why exactly is that?" Daniel knew there were probably a few books in Danato's library that would have been a beneficial read for him, but he rarely had to deal with werewolves, so he didn't really care to bore himself with them.

"Antiquated traditions," Nevia offered rather acridly.

"It's based on some incidents," Heaton corrected her diplomatically before explaining to Daniel. "They are concerned the fathers will hurt or even eat their children."

"Ridiculous," Nevia added with even more venom.

Heaton and Daniel glanced at her before Heaton continued. "Werewolves don't recognize humans as anything but food when they change. A werewolf baby in human form could be a temptation to them." Nevia opened her mouth to object with another point, but she huffed and shut up. "I agree that with the convenience of part-time caging, there really is no reason for Callin not to have rights to his child, but this is about more than a baby."

Nevia tapped her finger impatiently on her knee before putting her hands down to slip herself back down to the lower seat. Daniel touched her hand, a silent request for her to stay near him. She looked back. "I can't smell them as well between you two."

He gave her a nod of understanding and moved his hand. He turned to Heaton to ask him another question, but his grinning face was already looking at him. Daniel furrowed his brow at his jovial look.

"What's that about?" he asked.

Heaton shook his head and pressed his fingers to his lips. He settled back against the railing with Daniel and watched, though a remainder of the grin was still on his face.

The woman who had been glaring at Nevia stepped forward to speak. She introduced herself to Callin as Frederique Van Dorn. The name probably would have meant something to Daniel if he even remotely followed werewolf culture, but given the fact that there wasn't a Werewolf Weekly, and he really didn't care, he was left with only the assumption that she was somebody of importance. If he hadn't come to that conclusion by her introduction, he would have by Callin's modest head bow to her.

Frederique was attractive in that *every blonde you ever met* sort of way. Her only distinction was her height. He didn't prefer tall women, though he never made an exception to them either. For one night, he could handle just about any abnormal physique. Even a little extra tummy never bothered him as long as it came with an equally ample bosom.

She reminded him of Sophie, the way she stood strictly erect to show no shame in her height. Her chest was puffed up like a man's but without much to show for it. Her height left her with lean legs and even leaner breasts.

"Callin, we can all see that you care for your son greatly." Frederique began pacing before his cell. The thick heels she wore clomped on the polished white floor like horse hooves. "You are a rarity among our men."

"Only because you have conditioned us not to desire a bond with our offspring," Callin countered with discreet cynicism.

"Conditioned?" She gave herself a proper pause to appear as if she was thinking about it. "I think not. I think the male is far more intelligent than that, or don't you think so?" Callin didn't respond. There was no response to give that wouldn't persist in insulting his sex. "I think if the male of the species really cared about their offspring, there might be more incidents such as this."

"And how would I know if there were?" Callin didn't slam on the bars or snarl like Daniel might have expected from a male werewolf. He didn't even move from his civil stance. It was the same control that he saw in Ethan when he was in his guard uniform. This man was definitely an aberration from the usual image of male werewolves.

"Are you suggesting that the council would conceal information?"

"I'm not suggesting it. I'm outright saying it."

Frederique smiled and turned to her council for advisement. "Council, is there any truth to this statement? Do any of you remember previous trials regarding custody of children?" They all paused briefly, as if trying to recollect the past, and shook their heads. "There, you see? You are the first, Callin."

"Your evidence is astounding."

Frederique lost her smile, but the sneer that replaced it didn't seem to concern Callin.

"I don't have any quarrel with the council about the past. I only wish to proceed with the future. I want my son."

"You are gone nearly a week out of every month for your containment, and as you can see, you are currently incarcerated. How shall we begin to assess your reliability as a parent?"

"I'm not asking for sole custody. I only wish to be a part of my son's life."

"That's not what you were offering before, though. You kidnapped this child and wouldn't release him."

"I offered his mother the privilege of living with us."

"Offered? Privilege? I'm not sure where to start with that statement. Why would she wish to be ruled by a pseudo-pack?"

"Not ruled. *Ruler*. I offered her leadership. I asked her to be our matriarch queen."

There was a slight change of demeanor in the stands as the council took this in. Frederique glanced at the mother in question, as if this particular detail was not mentioned to her prior to the proceedings. The mother had taken no interest in the trial until then. The baby on her shoulder was still wailing, but she locked eyes with Callin. She apparently didn't expect that to come up.

"I offered her the rightful place in our *pseudo*-pack. As queen with dominion over my men, she would have had all of her children next to her, and all of her men to *help* care for those children." The word help seemed to stab the mother. She must have regretted not taking up his offer for that reason alone. The first child must have been a burden by itself, but the second was likely too much for her to handle with any measure of grace.

"The law strictly forbids packs, Callin. Offering a female leadership of one is beyond even the scope of civil disobedience. If Leona would have taken the title, then she would be in prison herself." Frederique made certain to glare at the woman before turning back to Callin. "I imagine that's why she didn't take up your offer."

"She didn't take up my offer because she was afraid of how much it appealed to her. All of you here today—" Callin spoke up a little to indicate the remainder of the Council of the Moon. "—you are here because you believe that you are the ruling body of the werewolf society, but the truth is, you are all being ruled, just as much as I and my fellow males are."

"Silence, you mutt," Frederique scolded.

"There is no ruling body, there is only the leader, and right now, *she* is the leader." Callin moved to point at Frederique.

At the same moment, Daniel felt a tap on his leg. He looked down and saw Nevia point in either direction for them to mobilize. He glanced at Heaton, who had gotten the same tap, and they parted ways.

"We are all being fooled into this regime," Callin continued to rant like a well-spoken presidential candidate.

Daniel slipped around the back of the bleachers as casually as he could. Heaton did the same on the opposite side and came to a stop close to the cell. If Frederique noticed his presence, she didn't react to it. As he came around the opposite side, he noticed that her upper lip was twitching in a canine snarl. All her rage was directed at Callin and about to blow.

"Once, we were free. Once, we considered any werewolf to be our kin. We didn't pit ourselves against each other: female against male, father against mother, clan against clan. The reigning Van Dorn family has been our dictatorship for nearly a century. *She* is the enemy to our children's future, not me." Callin jutted his finger at her again, and Frederique's already frayed temper broke. She grabbed his hand and clamped her teeth down on the accusing finger. When it gave way, she spat it to the floor.

Daniel cursed and rushed in without thinking. Heaton barked at him to stop, but he was already grabbing the fem-wolf from behind.

Of the many stupid things he had done in his life, attacking an angry fem-wolf was probably at the top of a lengthy list. She flipped him over her back the way he might have flipped a backpack off his back—a very light backpack at that.

He landed solidly against the floor without breaking any bones, but he had a little trouble getting his air. Lucky for him, she was more interested in removing more of Callin's digits. The man smartly backed deeper into his cell.

Heaton moved in front of Daniel to block her. A stupid choice on his part, but one that Daniel appreciated. Heaton had a tendency to make just as many stupid choices as Daniel, but they tended to work out to his benefit most of the time, so they usually got categorized as brave instead of stupid. This time, however, he got to add a notch to his stupid list.

When the fem-wolf had no target to nibble on, she turned back to Daniel and saw Heaton in her way. Her human hand whipped across his face. The backhanded slap sent him into the bleachers not far from the mother, Leona, who was gathering her oldest child closer to her for protection.

When Frederique stepped toward Daniel's supine body, he slid away with scrambling feet, but the cocking of Nevia's pistol stopped everything. Frederique broke her predatory gaze, and Daniel stopped floundering on the floor.

Nevia stood behind him with her gun held in both hands. Daniel glanced between the two women, trying to figure out if there was something he'd missed. Frederique seemed leery of the weapon, though she shouldn't have been. Bullets were hardly a deterrent to werewolves.

He could see the council bristling at the sight of their leader being threatened, but they were keeping their distance, either out of respect for the fight itself, or because Frederique hadn't asked them to join.

"I don't want to shoot you, Frederique. I'm only here to make sure this trial goes civilly."

"Careful, you might miss, and you don't want to know what I'll do to you for your impudence," Frederique snarled right back.

"She never misses." Daniel couldn't help but interject.

"Just settle down, and we can get back to the trial," Nevia said calmly.

"I'm not going to let this usurper undermine me. This trial is over. His rhetoric will not go beyond the confines of his cell. He has no right to his child, or his pack. Our laws are bound by strict edicts. We have no intention of bending them just because one man wants to be a daddy."

"He has that right!" Nevia yelled with just a hint of a childish tantrum behind it.

"Then he can have a half-breed with a human, just like your mother," Frederique seethed.

Daniel looked back at Nevia for confirmation of this, but she didn't meet his gaze. She looked hurt by the comment, more than angry. Daniel heard a low growl from Frederique, and he knew she was about to pounce on Nevia.

There was probably a point in time when he wouldn't have cared. There was probably a time when he would have considered Nevia responsible for her own actions, but that was not where he was now. Now he wanted to protect her, like all male minions of lust.

He assumed from the conversation that Nevia might know enough about the werewolf anatomy to wound her or kill her, but that would leave them with a long explanation for Danato, and he really didn't want that. Not to mention that shooting the highest-ranking member of the Council of the Moon was bound to incite the other fem-wolves, and then they would all be dead or severely dismembered.

There was a small chance he could stop this all without creating the type of damage he usually did. If he could do what Nevia had thought he might be able to do, then perhaps he could use both spectrums of his powers simultaneously. The result would hopefully be painful enough to Frederique to stop her, but not damaging enough to warrant an attack by the others, or reprimands for the use of his powers by Danato.

For the second time that day, he topped his stupid list. He jumped up and stood between Nevia and Frederique. Nevia yelled for him not to, but he didn't listen to her any more than he had to Heaton. Frederique seemed thrilled by the play toy placed before her and smiled maniacally.

He focused on the torrent of emotions he felt and activated the opposing spectrums of his power. The precursory energy usually prompted a warning for the transmorphs in his path. It was not pleasant, but it was as far as he could go without triggering the power. Even at partial strength, his power would strip her clothes and skin her alive before he could stop it.

He expected the same reaction as he always got—the straightening of the spine like she had been hit with an enormous blast of heat—but that wasn't the result. The power vibrated in his ears before he felt the detonation that threw him across the room.

He landed hard, sliding to a stop, and looked back at Frederique. He feared that his power had backfired, or worse, that he had somehow blown her up. She was across the room. She had been thrown in the opposite direction. She was struggling to rise from the floor.

He got to his feet with minimal difficulty. Nevia rushed to him with a dozen questioned molded into the expression on her face. He grimaced at her and shrugged. He didn't really know what he had done either.

Heaton moved to Frederique. He helped her up, though she seemed annoyed by the need for it. She panted, struggling to breathe, and she clenched her chest. She glared at Daniel as he approached with Nevia, who was unnecessarily supporting him by his right arm. "Are we done with this?" Daniel asked, playing like he had intended to do what he just did.

"We will adjourn for the day." Frederique was no doubt in a great deal of pain. He suspected that she either had cracked ribs or a collapsed lung, but so far, he seemed to be fine. He wondered if he had been farther away from her, whether he would have missed the bulk of the impact.

"I think that's a good idea," Daniel said.

"You might want to view the infirmary before you head back to your accommodations," Heaton offered, giving Daniel a furtive glance.

"Yes, I think you're right." Frederique also glanced at Daniel, but to his surprise, her expression held less anger than he'd expected. It must have been a good while since any man had bested her, let alone a human—albeit a disperser... but still. She seemed to recognize power as something to respect, even if it came from someone she might normally find beneath her. Respect was a hard thing to earn from a fem-wolf; he would have to try not to let it go to his head.

Heaton attempted to assist Frederique to the elevator, but she pushed him away in lieu of her fellow council members. Each of them lined behind her as if they were still the threatening stampede of beauty that they were when they entered, but their doubled-over leader had taken a good deal of the swagger from them.

Leona collected her babies and followed them, but Callin poked his arm through the bars. "Leona!" She paused before passing the three of them and looked back at him. "Is this what you really want, a bickering sister lording over you? She'll never give you the throne. She'll only give it to her daughters. None of them will be any fitter for it than she is."

Leona shook her baby to quiet it again, but it didn't work. "All I want now is to raise my babies."

"Alone?" He pressed his head into the bars. "Why are you being such a coward?" He seethed.

Leona glanced back at the three of them and they did their best to pretend they weren't watching the interaction intently, even though they clearly were.

"You are stronger than this. You could be more than just a single mother."

"The law doesn't allow it."

"*She* is the law! She tells us what to do! She dictates! She doesn't want a matriarchal society because she is already the matriarch of us!" Callin reached out his unbitten hand to touch her, but she stayed just out of reach. "You are the only one who can end this."

"I can't convince her…"

"I'm not asking you to convince her," Callin said sternly. "I'm asking you to overthrow her."

Leona shook her head.

"You could bring equilibrium back to our people. Don't you see how pathetic our species has become? We castigate the half-breeds of our clan, but we don't allow the full-bloods to be raised with the benefit of two parents. How can we demand purity of our race when we have no unity within it?"

Leona started to walk away.

"Fight, Leona! Fight for something, if not for me, then for our son. Fight for his right to be with the woman that he might someday love. Fight for your new daughter. Fight that she might have the right to be more than a footstool to Frederique, like you are."

Leona threw him a glare and continued to walk away. The baby wailed as she tromped past them.

"It's her leg," Nevia said as Leona passed. Leona whipped her head around to face her as she stopped. "The baby's leg is broken. That's why she won't stop crying."

"What?" Leona hissed. "How do you know that?"

"She smells of pain, her left leg is hanging limp, and she cries more after she is moved or tousled."

"You think I hurt my child?"

"I'm not saying that. Babies are fragile—even werewolf babies. It happens. I am merely suggesting that you stop by the infirmary to see your sister and have the doctor check it."

"I will not be told how to care for my child," she fumed.

"*I* don't tell people how to care for their children. That's the council's territory, isn't it?" Leona shuffled off, though with slightly less speed, since she seemed to sense the change in the child's pitch as she started moving again.

Heaton and Daniel exchanged looks and brought their attention to Nevia. A dozen or so questions leaped to Daniel's mind. Before he could ask them, Heaton and Nevia turned quizzical faces back on him. A dozen or so questions were on their minds as well, apparently. Before anyone could speak, Callin cleared his throat.

"I don't suppose anyone is interested in taking *me* to the infirmary." The werewolf looked pale as he held of his bloody finger out to them. He still had hope that it might be reattached. Fortunately, Frederique had not swallowed it. Thankfully, raw flesh was not nearly as appealing to werewolves while they were in human form.

It took a moment for Daniel to get the hint from Heaton and Nevia's dead stares that they expected him to do something about this. "This power is starting to suck," he grumbled before trying to save Callin's dismembered digit.

10

S OMEWHERE AMIDST THE TEARS, Cori had drifted off to sleep in Ethan's arms. She was surprised to find him still holding her when she woke up. She had apologized to him for everything, but none of that seemed to matter to him. All he wanted was to see her. That should have been a good thing, but she had a feeling it only meant that the issues from this new betrayal would come back to haunt her later.

She was about to force the issue when she heard a metallic tap on the door. They both looked over and saw Belus slip in through the still unlocked door with a pile of papers in his hands. The guards had either given up on keeping people out, or Belus didn't offer enough risk for them to bother. If they knew him better, they might still have let him in, but for different reasons.

He also closed it behind him to offer the appearance of privacy, even if there was none to be had. Cori removed herself from Ethan's arms and sat beside him on the bed. She was relieved and ecstatic to see Belus. She wanted to hug him, but as per his instructions, not to mention his abhorrence for her feminine zeal, she didn't. She did, however, give him a smile, which she hadn't been able to muster for anyone else. "Please tell me you have good news."

"I have information. I've already shared it with Danato. He's asked me to fill Ethan in, and since you're here..." Belus trailed off as he flipped through his papers.

"Seriously, I am the one sitting in jail here. Don't you think I have a right to know what's going on?"

Belus's eyes snapped back to her, and she realized she had said the wrong thing at the wrong time. "Right to know? *You* be serious, Cori. You aren't sitting in this jail cell for no reason. You let out three prisoners. This isn't something that was done to you. You chose this by not telling us about it first. Don't ask me to be honest and upfront with my information when you haven't been with yours."

Cori felt herself flush under Belus's reprimand. "I didn't think Danato would understand or agree with my urgency."

"Then you call *me*!" Belus yelled. It was a rare event, and even though it wasn't comparable to Danato's cacophonic bellows, it gave her pause. Belus glanced at Ethan as if he didn't want to speak in front of him.

Ethan leaned over and gave her a kiss on the check before getting up and heading to the door. "Ethan?" Cori asked, questioning his sudden abandonment.

His eyes flickered between them and settled on her. He shrugged. "You lied to us all, Cori."

She shook her head, but there was no denying it. Even if she could take back the crime of letting prisoners out, she'd still lied about the key.

"You can give any excuse you want about it, but the bottom line is you lied. I get that you didn't trust Danato. I get that you didn't want to pit me up against him. What about him?" He nodded to Belus. "He's your go-to guy now, isn't he? He's the one you can't even get pregnant without consulting." Belus raised a brow at that, but didn't interrupt. "Why *didn't* you call him?" Ethan slipped out, leaving her to face Belus alone.

It amazed Cori how quickly things in her life went from bad to worse. She'd thought Danato was going to be her biggest problem in all of this, but apparently not. "Well," Belus said after a moment. "Care to field that one?"

"I didn't call you, because..." Cori realized she hadn't really ever considered calling Belus. "I wasn't thinking clearly."

Belus shook his head. "That's a load of crap. You had calmed down enough to go search for a way to suppress Clark's men and plot the escape."

Cori sighed, knowing honesty was her only safety net in all of this. "I didn't even think to call you. I don't know why."

"I do." Belus tossed the files beside her. "Care to hear it?"

Cori sighed. It didn't matter if she cared to hear it or not. He was going to share, but she nodded obediently.

"It all goes back to that day you saved us from the elementals. You had to do it on your own. You didn't trust my plan, so instead of standing up for what you believed, you just slipped away and plotted one out yourself."

"Belus…" He didn't let her finish, but she didn't really have much to say after that, anyway.

"I'd like to say that you're selfish, and you want to just do everything by yourself, but I don't think that's it. I think you're just a coward. I think you would rather sit in this jail cell for making the choice to act alone than stand up for what you believe in and risk not getting it."

"So, I'm a selfish coward?" she offered with an eye roll. Belus stepped forward. For a moment, she thought he might slap her, but he threw his finger into her face.

"You want to continue this, or would you rather I leave without filling you in?"

She shook her head, feeling the sting of his reprimand like she was a child again. "No, sir," she managed to get out without crying.

"I don't think you're selfish, Cori." Belus pulled his finger back. "Quite the opposite; you're too compassionate. You see something wrong; you want to fix it. You see oppression, you want to alleviate it. The problem is that you don't take the long-term consequences into account. Not every situation is good versus evil. Whether you want to admit it or not, the elementals are dangerous beings. They needed to be assessed before any consideration for their release took place. I mean physiological *and* psychological. Yes, we've determined they were wrongfully imprisoned here, but with powers as great as theirs, freedom may not be the best choice for them either."

Cori nodded. Belus was making sense. She hated that. Clark was on one side of the good and evil spectrum by holding them against their will. Cori was on the other side by wanting to free them into the wild like they might suddenly become functional members of society. Naturally, Belus was somewhere in between. He understood that nothing in this place was yes or no, mostly it was just a lot of "maybes" with backup plans of "if all else fails."

"I should have gone to you," she mumbled at the realization of an unused ace in her hand.

"You should have told me about the key," Belus corrected. "You should have told me that Efrat made you doubt Danato." He sighed and looked around the cell. "Danato told me about his... threat." He paused, looking her over. "I really don't want to see you demoted. You have more to offer than that."

"I don't want that either."

"Ultimately, it might be his decision, but I can fight it if it comes to that." He put his finger back up in her face. "But if I do, I need to know you are with me, and not off on your own. I'm not like Danato, kid. I won't take you back. I might forgive, but I never forget."

Cori nodded.

"No more secrets involving prisoners or anything that sounds remotely suspicious to you."

"Yes, sir." Cori looked at the door to see if the guards were close by. They were perched by the door within earshot. When she looked back, Belus was tipping his head in confusion. He could already sense her unrest with her secret.

"What is it?"

"Nothing, I just..." Cori wanted to tell him everything, but she wasn't sure yet. She needed to hear his news first. She wanted to know the plan before she showed all her cards. "I'm sorry, Belus." After a moment of tentative pawing on his shirt, she reached her arms around his waist and hugged him. She heard him sigh in exasperation, but he didn't push her away.

"Damn you, kid," he grumbled. "Of all the women Danato could have brought here, why did he have to pick such an affectionate one?"

"I'm not *that* affectionate," she muttered into his side. "I just have to make up for your hostility."

He grumbled an acknowledgment and, after a second or two of pause, he put his hand on the back of her head, almost petting her. "Hey," he whispered, and she looked up at him, "what was that about you getting pregnant?"

She pulled away from him with a sigh. "Ethan wants to have a baby," she said in equally hushed tones. "I told him I would have to check with you first."

Belus glanced toward the door. "Why?"

She shrugged. "Hell, if I know. It might turn my hair to snakes, it might cause a plague, or turn everyone's left shoe inside out. I just figured I should consult with you before I did."

He grunted another wordless response and moved his papers so he could sit beside her. "So, releasing prisoners, not a phone call, but the private lives of you and your husband you need help with."

Cori furrowed her brow.

"Are you sure you weren't just using me as an excuse?"

She shrugged.

"Do you *want* to have a baby?"

She crossed her arms. "You're the second man to ask me that this week, and you're the second man I don't have an answer for."

Belus smiled. "That's okay, we have less difficult issues to attack right now, but in case it makes a difference, I have no objections to a child. A few precautions spring to mind, but don't let that stop you."

Cori nodded. She wasn't sure Belus's approval was going to make the decision any easier, and in fact, knowing that everyone else was on board without her might have just scared her further from the idea, but it was nice to know the option was there if she wanted to go through with it.

11

Daniel thought he had benefited from not passing out after healing Callin, but the heat wave that had him undressing in the elevator was enough to make him wish he had. "Feck, it's hot in here," he said, pulling off his shirt.

"We'll get you outside in just a minute." Heaton grabbed his hands before he could undo his trousers.

Daniel panted and pressed his face against the cool metal of the elevator. He thought the metal might melt from the heat he was casting off, but instead, the metal maintained its cool feel. If he hadn't been too delirious to judge, he would have sworn it felt colder the longer he pressed against it.

When the doors *ponked*, he ran out toward the foyer and the exit door, leaving friends, shoes, socks, and shirt in his proverbial dust. He slammed open the door to the outside fall air, which for the artic climate might as well have been winter. He groaned with relief as he lobbed his body into a left-over snow drift.

He couldn't claim that the snow sizzled on contact, but he felt himself slip down a little from the immediate melting. It was probably not wise for him to change temperatures so quickly, but he imagined his abilities came with the appropriate bodily compensations for it. He let out another groan as Nevia and Heaton came out to join him in full winter wear.

Heaton clutched his coat, while Nevia carried his clothes. She looked him over as she approached. "You shouldn't do that. You could burn your skin."

"On snow?"

"You know what I mean. Sudden temperature change isn't good for the capillaries in your skin." She hugged herself. Despite his warning, she still hadn't brought the best coat. She was still too interested in fashion to comprehend what real cold was about. The navy wool pea coat must have kept her warm in her U.S. winters, but it was useless here.

"Cold?" he asked with a grin. "I'll warm you up." He motioned for her to come to him. She glanced at Heaton, who shook his head with empathy for his friend's endless innuendos.

"I'm going to the house," she announced as she backed away. "Hurry up, you'll need water," she called as she stomped off.

Daniel couldn't help but smile after her. He found some amusement in the fact that she seemed to hate the cold as much as he hated the heat. He supposed that was just one sign they were a horrible match, followed quickly by their age difference, their conflicting temperaments, and a few other things that he was still trying to figure out.

When he looked back at Heaton to make a joke about her being a cold fish, he saw a cheeky smile glaring back at him. Daniel furrowed his brow and pulled his head back like Heaton's beaming lips had actually struck him. He twirled his finger at his face. "What is that wick about?"

"What's with you two? I think you almost made her blush."

"Really?" Daniel looked after her like he might actually see the difference between rosy frost-bitten cheeks and blushing cheeks. Heaton laughed and offered him a hand up. Daniel took it.

"You do realize you're hopelessly in love with her, don't you?" Heaton said as he draped Daniel's coat over his shoulders. He wasn't completely cooled down yet, but the snow melting against his pants was bringing in a quicker temperature drop than his nether region needed.

"That's bullocks. I just like teasing her."

"You don't even see it yet," Heaton said, ushering him forward with firm pressure to the back.

"See what?"

"The frustration, the confusion, the obsession." Daniel shook his head, not grasping the connection. "Don't you remember the state Ethan was in when he was hung up on Cori, but figured she didn't want him, or *did* want him but was too hung up on her dead lover to consider letting herself have him?"

Daniel stopped. "Are you elephants or just a gobshite? This…" Daniel motioned between him and the long since gone Nevia. "…is not the same thing. She's my partner. We just work together. That is bound to cause a little sexual tension."

"Hmm, and explain to me how that is any different from what Ethan and Cori are to each other."

Daniel scoffed and moved on. "I am not burying my head in the bottle and wailing in a drunken fit over some bird."

"No, you're doing quite the opposite. You're keeping your head out of the bottle and making an effort to be less of an ass over some bird."

"I am *not* less of an ass!" Daniel spat before he realized how ridiculous the statement was. "And I skipped out on one night of alcohol. That doesn't mean I'm trading my yockers to suck up to some scanger. If anyone here is in love with her, it's you."

"Me!" Heaton chuckled. "How, may I ask, did you come to that conclusion?"

"Oh, come on—the cigarettes, the avoidance, that little conversation while you two were lurching on the dance floor. Tell me you didn't just finally admit your true feelings to her."

Heaton chuckled again. "Well, you got me there, Daniel, but no, I'm not in love with her."

Daniel stopped and stared at him. "You know you're killing me right now with this secret stuff."

Heaton tipped his head as if he couldn't quite understand what Daniel was talking about.

"You're supposed to be *my* partner, not hers. Damn, that sounded poof. You know what I mean."

"I know. I thought we were all partners."

"Yeah, but not like us. Five years, man. Isn't that something? Isn't that worth sticking around for?"

Heaton took in a deep breath and Daniel saw the sympathy he had otherwise been lacking. "I'm sorry I said what I said. I was protecting myself prematurely, and as I can see now, immaturely." Heaton crossed his arms and looked down at his feet as if they held his next line. "I'm not going to transfer. I—"

Daniel interrupted him with a hug. Heaton laughed and undid his arms to hug him back. He only offered a light pat on the back, but Daniel gave him the full brotherly squeeze that somehow didn't seem as touching when the other person couldn't breathe.

When he pulled back, he realized he might have made an already touching moment into a full-blown after-school special. "Good. I'm glad. Cause you can't leave me alone with her. She's freaking nuts." Daniel kept walking. "She looks at me like I'm a freaking lab experiment. I swear, if she could take my blood and look at it under a microscope, she would." Heaton walked on with him, but notably a half-step behind him. "I think she may try to remove my brain while I'm sleeping."

"Have you slept with her yet?"

Daniel paused in his step, giving away the answer to the question. "It doesn't matter. She doesn't want me, Heaton."

"What's that?" Heaton said with mock shock as they reached the front door of the house. "A woman doesn't want an oversexed, near-alcoholic man with anger issues and a criminal past? That perplexes me." Daniel glared at him and reached for the doorknob, but Heaton stopped him. "How many women do you suppose could handle being shouted at by Danato without being brought to tears?"

"Women? Feck that, the man brings tears to *my* eyes."

"Right, so maybe your past, your powers, and your acerbic personality won't scare her away. There are probably a few things that she's running away from, but it's not that. Figure out what it is that's keeping her away and work on that."

"Why would you encourage this? You know I'm shit with women. This could make our work life hell."

"So, we don't invite her to the bar after you break up. Just go for it. A proper relationship would be good for you."

"Why?" Daniel was pretty sure he would give him a laundry list of reasons why he should open his heart to the right person, but Heaton just pushed up the sleeve of his coat and shirt to show his healed arm.

"Because that's fucking amazing, and if she was willing to be your damn pincushion to get this out of you, then that's the type of girl you change your life for." Heaton headed in and shut the door, leaving Daniel to ponder that statement for a bit, as well as finish cooling off.

12

WHEN CORI AND BELUS finished their discussion, he called Ethan back in to go over the paperwork he had brought in. Ethan sat down beside her, hunched over his knees. Intentionally or otherwise, the position offered little room for contact. She pushed herself back against the wall to sit Indian-style and ignored the offence.

"Dr. Jillian Frank," Belus went on, handing Ethan a copy of Jill's file, which apparently had made it in on the latest delivery. Cori wondered how fast they would have gotten the information if they didn't live outside of the information age. "As Cori said, she was the doctor who created the elementals. She was hired by the American military to transplant the hands of recorded supernatural beings to volunteer military soldiers. They believed the hands were the source of the power, and therefore the power could be transferred along with the hands."

Ethan handed her the document, and she looked at the picture of Dr. Frank, but she passed the paper right back. The only image she had left of this woman was of her head being whipped back by a bullet. Ethan must have caught the paper right back. The only image she had left of this woman was of her head being whipped back by a bullet. Ethan must have caught her discomfort because he changed positions so that he could put his hand on her leg.

"First Sergeant Efrat Alston was pulled off special ops to be the leading member of the planned 'super team.' He was one of General Clark's favorites."

"Efrat might have mentioned he was in special ops. It's hard to remember. We were trying to kill each other during that conversation." Cori wasn't sure that deemed mentioning, but she needed to pry herself out of the hole she had dug herself, and that was only going to happen with complete translucency. She had been working toward that with Ethan, but she had obviously slid back down a very steep hill… into a hole… with quicksand. As it was, she was still holding back, and she knew she needed to get out quick before she lost her job, her mentor, and possibly her marriage.

"He was a decorated officer. Well respected and devoted to his career in the military."

Cori took the new file on Efrat that offered a brief history of his service record and a much younger, much prouder picture of him. She now had two interpretations of Efrat in her head. She wasn't sure which one was accurate—maybe both, or maybe neither. Six years was a long time to gather bitterness and resentment. Those were hard emotions to let go of.

"Corporal Paul Hirem was also a loyal soldier. He was expected to do great things."

Ethan looked at the document and handed it to her, but she turned away and shook her head. She didn't need to see his face. She already had enough memories of his face in her mind. Memories that were not her own, and yet too close to not be a part of her.

She could see Belus exchanging a look with Ethan, but she didn't care. They didn't understand and they never would. Right now, Cleos was the only person who understood how she felt about Hirem and Jill, and he wasn't likely to help her through it. He wasn't likely to speak to her ever again.

"Remi and Garrett, or Garr as we all know him, were privates. They were barely out of boot camp when they were brought into the experiment."

Ethan glanced at both the files, but didn't hand them to her.

"So, what do we know now that we didn't know earlier?" Cori asked, getting slightly impatient.

"We know that Jill lost her license to practice medicine three years ago. She was making a big stink about the disappearance of her patients and a smoke screen was deployed to get her to shut up. She went bankrupt seemingly overnight, and was forced to fall back on her lesser-known skills of singing. She never stopped searching for them. She kept in contact with several people inside the government and the military. She must have known that they were taken to our prison, but she didn't know how to get to us, and I doubt she had any idea what we do here."

"She didn't," Cori said. "She didn't care, either. She only came here to finish what she didn't have the heart to do six years ago. She came to kill Hirem and herself. I guess she accomplished it."

"Yes, she did," Belus said in a wary tone. "The point of all this is that the board now knows the reason for their incarceration. They are weighing in on what to do about that. As far as the military goes, they are out. They are in breach of contract. Their rental agreement is revoked."

"So is Cori free?" Ethan asked, grabbing her hand.

"Not, yet," Belus said. "The military wants the elementals back. They are claiming them as property. We are claiming Cori as our property. Basically, they are holding her for collateral at this point."

"Danato's going to send the collectors out, isn't he?" Cori asked.

Belus huffed and walked over to the door to check on the guards. They had moved away from the door, per Ethan's request, but they were still walking around the hall outside.

Satisfied with the level of privacy they had, Belus returned. "Cori, the collectors were sent out last night twenty minutes after you were dragged off. Danato didn't tell Clark that, because he needed to find out why you had released them. You may not have trusted him to do the right thing, but he trusted that you had."

Cori looked down, feeling the burden of reality pulling her from her fairy tale world, as Efrat not so lovingly referred to it. She may have known Danato well, but Efrat was right that he would put the prison first no matter what request she made to the contrary. She was glad that Danato wasn't telling Clark about it, though. That was something, anyway.

"Will the board grant the elementals asylum?" Cori asked, looking up from her mope.

"I don't know. I can guarantee they won't let them go," Belus pointed out, to clarify that freedom was still not an option.

"I don't care about that. I'm not interested in their freedom and frankly, neither are they. They already know that's a long shot at best. All I want to know is if you think with enough sweet talk that you can get them out of Clark's clutches."

Belus's brow furrowed, and Ethan turned to her to examine her sudden change in demeanor. "They will be assessed, as I said, but if they are going to be contained for any crimes, it will be for the deaths of our guards, and that sentence will be carried out by us, not Clark."

"Can you promise me that?" she asked, just to make certain he wasn't blowing smoke.

Belus arched an eyebrow and glanced at Ethan. "Can you tell me why you're asking?"

Cori bit back her lips for a moment. "Promise me they won't be gunned down by Clark like Jill and Hirem."

Belus raised his chin resolutely. "I promise." Cori leaned back, feeling a weight lift from her shoulders. Somehow, a promise from Belus was as good as a signed, stamped, and delivered pile of paperwork. "Cori?" His voice impressed upon her a question that needed to be answered. She didn't wait for him to ask it.

She glanced at the door and leaned forward again. Both men instinctively imitated her to get in on the intrigue. "I haven't been completely honest about the way I helped the elementals escape." Belus took in a deep breath, like he needed to keep his temper in check. Cori glanced at Ethan, fearing he might be just as angry, but his eyes were wide as he waited for her to speak. "Don't be mad," she whispered. Her brow knitted in dreaded anticipation of the impending bombshell.

Belus's eyelids lowered to slits. "I'm already mad. How much worse can it get?"

13

"SHE *WHAT*?" DANATO SLAMMED his fists into his desk, making the metal creak. Ethan and Belus stood before him reporting the news of Cori's new betrayal, or perhaps it was an un-betrayal, but either way, it was another lie. Ethan looked stunned and distant from the conversation. Belus, as usual, was calm, but he looked weary despite being the only one who had gotten a decent amount of sleep last night.

"She assumed without the delay of their discovery she wouldn't have time to convince us they aren't the danger we thought they were."

Danato bristled, listening to Belus report to him facts that Cori should have delivered directly to him. He hated being the last to know, especially when Belus was the first to know. "Where the hell are they?"

Belus paused and Danato glared at him, challenging him to withhold anything Cori had said. "The greenhouse," Ethan mumbled. "She's smart. Even if the collectors had been released onsite, their scent would have been disguised by the plants. Not to mention she's the only one who goes in there."

Danato could hear the pride in his voice, but it didn't show on his face. He was doubly exhausted by this runaround. Danato had been concerned from day one that Ethan's relationship with Cori would put a strain on his duties. He only hoped that the added stress didn't make him change how he felt about her.

"Yes, Cori is clever," Danato conceded, letting his fists unclench. "Too clever sometimes," he muttered.

"Cori has implored us not to reveal their location to Clark until we can be sure that we can protect them." Danato knew he was glaring at Belus, but he couldn't help it. "She would have told you, but she wanted to make sure that asylum was a probability rather than a possibility."

"And is this the type of behavior you condone in your successor, Belus?"

Belus paused, taking in that comment. "Not at all, but then again, I tend to feel that last night was doomed to failure the minute you invited a band to a top-secret prison." Danato's upper lip twitched. "I don't suppose anyone's given any attention to how Dr. Frank was able to just march right upstairs and shoot two guards in pursuit of her murder suicide. If we're going to start throwing blame for bad behavior, I would start there."

"Is that so?" Danato maintained an even voice. He was about to formulate a response to that scathing accusation when the door to the office slammed shut. Ethan had walked out. Danato furrowed his brow.

Belus and Danato exchanged glances before they headed out, once again partnered by their duties.

14

E THAN WASN'T ABOUT TO hang around and listen to Danato and Belus bark about who is the bigger fool. The bottom line was that they were all fools. Ethan had mistakenly assumed that with Cleos out of her life, Cori would confide in him when she was in trouble. Unfortunately, in asking her to not make him choose between his job and her, he had essentially told her to do just the opposite.

As mad as he was for giving her mixed messages, he was furious at Belus and Danato for doing the same. Danato presented himself as this stalwart leader demanding her to be disciplined and forthcoming, but when push came to shove, he was as rebellious and closed-mouthed as her. Belus should have been the solution. He should have been the mentor she needed, but he could never be the hero she needed.

The only hero Cori needed was Ethan, and he was about to fill that role in spades.

15

B Y THE TIME DANATO and Belus had caught up with Ethan, he was already outside, heading to the military barracks to find Clark. Danato had considered this route himself, but he wouldn't act on it unless he thought Cori's freedom was truly in danger.

"Ethan," Danato called after him, but he didn't slow or turn around. Belus was already lagging behind, not willing to give chase. As it was, Danato's cane wasn't doing well on the icy path. "Ethan!"

Ethan slowed and finally stopped.

"What are you doing?"

"I'm finishing this. The way it should have been finished the minute Clark burst into our home."

It didn't surprise Danato that Ethan was second-guessing him. The night before, when everything had gone amiss, he didn't have a chance to gauge the situation for himself. Now, with Cori facing another night in jail and her future on the precipice, he was panicking. He wasn't looking to Danato for the answers anymore, but he also wasn't looking at the broader picture.

"What are you doing?"

"I want Cori out of there," Ethan seethed.

"So do I, but she did—"

"I don't give a fuck about that!"

Belus strolled up beside Danato, catching Ethan's eye.

"If you two could stop bickering for a minute, you would see how simple this is."

Danato crossed his arms and waited for Ethan to say it.

"Clark wants the elementals in exchange for Cori. Let's just make the trade."

"And that will fix everything, will it?" Danato asked.

"It will get her out of there."

"I'm not so sure about that. Clark isn't a man known for negotiating."

"We shouldn't have to be negotiating to begin with." Ethan looked away. His frustration was near the tipping point. He only needed a good excuse to blow. "Why are we cavorting with this guy at all? He has no right to hold Cori. We've revoked his rental agreement, so let's kick him out."

"Belus is working on that," Danato said evenly.

"Why do we need paperwork to do that? Let's just do it! Is this really just about her learning a lesson?"

Danato sighed. He hated being the bad guy all the time. Luckily, Belus stepped up to bat for him. "Ethan, she assumed the responsibility of letting three prisoners out. She knew what the potential consequences would be."

"So, it's okay for Clark to shoot one of his prisoners without any consequences?"

"Yes, it is." Belus's quick response temporarily curtailed Ethan's dispute. He wasn't expecting that to be his answer. "The legalities of the outside world don't apply here. We run by our own code of ethics to match the necessity."

"I have at times executed prisoners," Danato added. "You know that."

"That's not the same," Ethan said, running his fingers through his hair.

"I suppose you have no bias against our code of ethics," Danato pointed out, "being as, on paper, you are technically my slave."

Ethan shook his head. He wasn't sure how to respond to that.

"My point is, we already operate outside of universal edicts. If we didn't follow any protocols, then we'd be in chaos."

"I understand that. I'm willing to uphold those protocols, but my obedience to them ends the second Clark tries to extradite Cori. I won't let him take her."

"Neither will I. Neither will Belus," Danato added, offering Belus a glance that he nodded in agreement to. "We need to fix this through protocol. This isn't just about Cori anymore. This situation is more than I can write off with a simple report. Losing a major rental income is a lot to ask from people who already contribute healthy donations to keep this place running properly."

Ethan took another moment to look at the landscape. "If we haven't found any legal means to free her by tomorrow night, I'm going to take Clark up on his offer."

"Say again?" Danato wasn't entirely sure what he was hearing, so he wanted to be sure before he reacted.

Ethan looked back at him. His expression was a little sad, and a little tired, but unyielding. "If Cori isn't home by suppertime tomorrow night, I'm going to give Clark the elementals."

Danato couldn't quite muster the strength to yell. He wasn't as angry as he thought he would be at hearing Ethan outright defy him. It was his first time in doing so, so it took him a moment to calculate what he was feeling. His eagerness to have Cori back quelled part of his temper, but it was his disappointment that dampened his ferocity. Cori was once again splitting Ethan's loyalties, and Danato was losing.

"Give me one good reason that I shouldn't throw you in a cell right beside her for that threat."

Ethan moved toward him and Danato naturally puffed his chest and tensed his muscles. When Ethan settled into his military stance before him, he relaxed. "I'm not threatening you, Danato. I'm making a decision."

"It's not your decision to make."

"Then why am I here? Why did you bring me here?" Ethan looked around the grassy, snow-patched grounds.

"Why did you train me? When did you suppose I should start making command decisions?"

"When I say." Danato crossed his arms. It was a typical parental response, but the truth was, he didn't know when. Ethan had long since been given the duties of a warden, but when it came to the major decisions and catastrophes, Danato always took the reins.

"Bottom line is, Danato, I'm not letting my wife sit in that jail cell one more night. I'm not concealing that plan from you, but I'm also not asking permission. You can continue to negotiate as it pleases you, but I have no loyalties to the elementals. If it's between them and her, it's going to be them."

Ethan stalked back the way they had come, and Danato felt his anger rise. He was grappling for a hold on his vocabulary when Belus spoke up.

"What about Cori's loyalties?" Belus asked.

The question stopped Ethan's crunching boots.

"What about her loyalties?" he asked. They all turned once again to face each other. For a moment, the question hung between them.

"She did all of this to save them, Ethan," Belus said in an even tone that Danato couldn't have faked if he tried. "As stubborn as she is, don't you think she'll be a little perturbed to find out you just handed them over to their executioner? Why do you think Danato and I are bickering so hard over this?"

Danato perked up at the question. He was curious about the answer himself.

"Neither of us gives a shit about them. Honestly, they are a huge burden on the facility and I would be happy to be rid of them. But for reasons not entirely clear to us, Cori feels obligated to help them. We, in turn, feel obligated to help her help them. Everything she's done up to this point is putting us at odds with a simple conclusion."

Belus paused, glancing at Danato. "Cori's behavior warrants a full demotion. The fact that she didn't actually release the elementals isn't going to work in her favor, since it was just another layer of deception to keep them out of our custody. When this is all over, neither one of us is going to want to punish Cori."

Danato couldn't help but stare blankly at Belus as he told him exactly what he was feeling.

"It's my job to blame the entire night on Danato's reckless use of funds, so we claim Cori as a victim of circumstances beyond her control. It's Danato's job to blame me for negligence, so we can't hold her responsible for my errors in judgment."

Danato glanced at Ethan, and he could see he wasn't the only one surprised by Belus's insight.

"You see, Ethan, we are all after the same goal. We want Cori to be safe and happy. If you turn the elementals over to Clark, it will be *you* she's aiming daggers at, not us."

Ethan looked down at his feet. He didn't take Belus's lectures well—he never had—but once in a while, they could see eye to eye. It wasn't usually about Cori, but there was a first for everything.

"Watching her in there has to be ten times easier than watching her through a transmorph," Belus added when Ethan didn't concede right away. "If you could keep your cool through that, you can keep your cool through this."

Ethan nodded, finally offering some modicum of retreat from his previous statement. "I just need to fix this."

"Ethan," Danato chimed back in, "I want to remove her from that cell with every fiber of my being. I've even considered it."

"You don't show it," Ethan mumbled snidely.

"I can't fall apart. It's easy to get angry, because everyone is used to that from me, but the control I exert through that anger is what is important. So, with a heavy heart and an extremely tight grip on my anger, I implore you not to disobey me on this. I want Cori in that cell, and the elementals hidden, until I get full permission from the board to do otherwise. Then all hell will break loose and you can save your damsel in distress with me as your sidekick."

Ethan sighed. He obviously didn't want to comply, but he was still Ethan, and as much as he wanted to have Cori back, he still couldn't bring himself to break from his self-defined character. "Yes, sir."

16

After Ethan calmed down, Danato suggested he go back in to see Cori. Even if he couldn't save her, he could at least comfort her.

There wasn't any discussion between him and Belus prior to deviating from the path back to the prison entrance. It went without saying that they needed to check up on their missing residents in the greenhouse.

The fans in the greenhouse hummed loudly in the humid building. The smell of dirt, fertilizer, and vegetation reminded Danato of Cori. She had been in and out of this building so much, it had become her signature scent.

The aroma brought on a twinge of guilt, but he wasn't sure why. Perhaps he blamed himself for this happening more than he realized. When it boiled down to it, Danato was responsible for all of this. If he had been doing his job properly, the elementals would never have been accepted as prisoners. Everything up to this point, including the death of so many guards, could be blamed on his blind grief.

"Efrat!" Danato boomed over the fans. He couldn't see any of them, but he knew they were there. The hairs on his arms were standing on end. "It's time to talk."

"Just talk?" Danato and Belus turned at hearing Efrat's voice behind them, but he wasn't there. "I wasn't sure you were capable of that." The fans muffled his voice, but it echoed through the space.

"Not usually, but we both know how persuasive Cori can be." Danato waited for an answer. Behind him, a pair of boots landed on the concrete path. Danato looked back and then up at the rafter Efrat had dislodged himself from.

Efrat's hands danced with an electrical threat as he emerged from his crouched position. Danato noticed his sleeves were covered in blood—transferred from the victims or Cori, he wasn't sure which.

Belus abruptly turned away. Garr and Remi must have come up from the rear, but Danato didn't take his eyes off Efrat. He wanted to see what Cori saw, but he couldn't. This man was cold and calculating. He would never be able to forgive him for almost killing her, even if she could.

"I don't understand it," Danato said, not making any sudden moves. Despite his indignation, he knew how dangerous Efrat was. Cori hadn't begun to fathom the extent of his power. The fact that he showed a modicum of control when attacking his men was the only reason Danato hadn't demanded his execution long ago. It was the only leniency he cared to offer him.

"Don't understand what?" Efrat asked, already uninterested in the conversation.

"I don't understand what redeeming quality she sees in you."

Efrat lowered his hands and directed them backward as a gesture of good faith. He looked like he was skiing without poles, but given Danato's new understanding of his predicament, he understood he didn't have the option to just pocket his hands. The others must have done the same, because he saw Belus relax.

"She's just a princess trying to make this place a pretty pink palace." Efrat smiled.

"That princess is risking everything to protect you. You might want to show her a little more respect."

"Is she... protecting us?"

"We're unarmed and without guards, or Clark, so what does that tell you?"

"It tells me that you're stupid. It tells me that you're wrapped around her little finger."

Danato narrowed his eyes at the suggestion of weakness. He wanted to prove his strength, but once again, muscles didn't necessarily beat lightning. "It also tells me we have a chance."

"What do you want, Efrat? And I only ask so that we understand each other. I'm not opening this meeting up for negotiations."

Efrat looked behind him to his partners. "We want asylum from Clark and the United States military. We will agree to stay confined, for now, as long as we are given proper care."

"What does *for now* mean?"

Efrat took in a breath. "When this is all over, when you're satisfied that all is well, I would like to discuss... options."

"Options for what? Your release?"

"That will be part of the discussion."

Danato waited, seeing Efrat's reluctance to speak, as if he were ashamed of the humility he had to express in asking for what he wanted. "We would like to discuss medical options." His jaw clenched like he didn't want to say the rest. "We—some of us are considering amputation." The word made his face distort with disgust.

Danato finally afforded a look back to Garr and Remi. Garr looked unexpressive, as usual, but his head was low. Remi was standing tall and proud, like the military had taught her, but her eyes were streaming with tears. In a different moment, he might have been inclined to feel sympathy, but at that moment, he was still focused on the task at hand.

"I assume that would alleviate the powers?" Danato asked, turning back to Efrat.

"Yes," Efrat said, glaring. "The hands are all that control the power. That's why we can't shut them off. They have no connection to our natural minds. We have virtually no control other than high and low."

"Removing your hands would prevent you from being a danger to society, but I can't overlook the death of so many of my men."

"You can put us on trial for that if you like. All I can do is refer back to my previous statement: virtually... no... control."

"As you said, we can deal with all of that once we get through this melee. I assume you can continue to hide here while we sort things out. It may be another day."

Efrat nodded. "That's it? Just like that? I ask for asylum and you grant it."

"No, of course not." Danato furrowed his brow. "*Cori* asked for your asylum. I couldn't give a damn what you want, but as you said, she has me wrapped around her finger. Good thing for you." He couldn't help but snarl as he walked past Efrat, with Belus only slightly behind.

"Is she alright?" Efrat asked as they reached the plastic curtain.

Danato turned back to look at him, but Efrat didn't offer his face. He considered walking out without offering him the satisfaction of relieving his conscience. "She's fine."

"Any more episodes?" he asked.

Danato exchanged a look with Belus. "How do you mean?"

Efrat turned back, his face painted with something that might have been sympathy if it was on someone else's face. "She didn't take Hirem's death well."

"Cori isn't particularly fond of seeing people die in front of her. It's a little thing she has," Danato offered, more sarcastically than he intended.

"Yes, but Jill's knowledge..." Efrat's eyes searched them like he was trying to find something. Then he suddenly dropped his search and shrugged. "I just wouldn't advise leaving Cori alone in a room with Clark, especially if he's unarmed." He smirked slightly and let his eyes fall away in thought. "Though that may not matter," he mumbled and turned around.

Danato couldn't tell if Efrat was manipulating them or if he really knew something they didn't. He hoped it was just the details he witnessed last night and not another deception from Cori.

17

As soon as Daniel had hung his coat up, Nevia set a glass of water on the island for him to drink. He felt naked without his shirt, but he found it over the head chair at the dining table and slipped it on. He didn't bother buttoning it before guzzling down the glass of water. For the most part, the water made it into his mouth, but since his ass was already wet, he didn't care how much he dribbled on his chest.

When he finished the glass and set it down, Nevia handed him a new glass full to the brim. He took about half of that down before his thirst was quenched enough to sip on the rest. Nevia filled the first glass again and stared at him. He glanced at Heaton, who was on the opposite side of the island, sitting on a stool. He was also watching him.

"Are we doing an intervention or what?"

Nevia crossed her arms, which gave her otherwise unobtrusive cleavage a boost. He did his best not to enjoy the view too much, but he already had her on his radar for her display with Danato. There wasn't a lot of hope for gentlemanly behavior.

"Are you going to tell us what happened in there?" she asked.

"His finger's back on, isn't it? I'll fix the scar later."

"No, not that." Nevia scowled like his daftness was diminishing her patience. He didn't think that was quite fair, since his brain was probably just as overheated as his body. "The thing with Frederique."

"Oh, that." His interest dimmed.

"What did you do?"

He opened his mouth wide and leaned over the island. Nevia naturally lowered herself with him, like he was about to reveal a big secret. "I have no idea."

She scoffed and straightened up.

"Don't be haughty about it. I don't exactly come with an instruction manual."

"Do you remember what you did?" Heaton asked.

"Yeah, sort of. I mean, I could duplicate it."

"Why didn't it make your temperature change?" Nevia asked. "You seemed fine afterward, apart from being thrown across the room."

"I think it was because I used both sides of the power simultaneously," Daniel said as he searched the fridge for edible food.

"You did it? You used *both*?" Nevia's eyes widened as if she might jump for joy if he gave her the right answer.

"Look at her." Daniel nodded to Heaton. "It's like fecking Christmas for her."

"What was it like? What did it feel like?"

Daniel pulled out the fixings for a sandwich and set it on the island. "You saw what it did. It felt like somebody punched me in the chest. Heaton, you want a sandwich?"

"Yeah, man."

"Daniel," Nevia whined.

"Calm down, I'll make you one too," he said, knowing full well what her whine was for.

"No, that's not—"

"With cheese or without?" He waved a plastic-wrapped piece of cheese in her face before she could continue.

"What… no." She ripped the cheese from his hand and set it down on the counter. "Tell me what you did!"

Daniel glanced at Heaton and offered him a smirk. "Tell me about what Frederique said to you."

"Yeah." Heaton stood and smirked back at him as he came around to Nevia's other side. "She said your mother was a half-breed. Does that mean she was half werewolf, half human?"

Nevia looked between them, but didn't answer. Daniel approached her left flank. "So, grandma got it on with a werewolf."

She glared at that remark, but didn't respond.

"That means you're technically one quarter werewolf," Heaton said, leaning against the stove. "That's where you get the sense of smell."

"My olfactory abilities *exceed* even werewolves," Nevia snapped defensively.

"What else do you do?" Daniel looked her body up and down. "Do you howl at the moon?"

Nevia ignored the jibe and stared out into the living room as they continued their mockery.

"Are your fingernails as hard as nails?" Heaton asked.

"Do you have to wax your back?" Daniel asked with a scrunched-up face of sympathy.

"You don't run well for a werewolf," Heaton pointed out.

"And you're kind of scrawny," Daniel added, pinching her slender biceps.

"Yes, but I am still armed." Nevia pulled her pistol from its holster under her arm.

"Oh, that's right," Heaton said, drawing himself back. "I keep forgetting there's a reason we don't tease you."

Daniel looked over the gun in her hand. He wanted to make a comment about the gun only making her more attractive to him, but he needed to not get into all that again. She had cut him deep with her accusations, and if only to prove to her he could, he wanted to make it through the rest of this trip without acting on his baser instincts.

"Was that a yes or no on cheese?" he asked, not being able to hide his smile of admiration.

"I can make them," she said suddenly, holstering her gun like she was rude not to have offered already. She liked to help, and normally he would have loved to have a woman prepare food for him, but she was already a cute gun-toting demi-wolf. If she added kitchen skills to that list, he was liable to drag her home and introduce her to his mother.

She reached for the bread and he grabbed her hand and pulled it away. "I can handle sandwiches, but if you want, you can get Heaton a beer." Nevia pulled her hand back, and he squeezed it before letting go. He probably *did* need an intervention. He was stuck in an endless circle of attraction, friction, and dissatisfaction with the only woman he had ever slept with twice, and he was addicted to it.

Nevia pulled three beers out of the fridge. She popped the top off one and offered it to Daniel as he prepared the sandwiches. He shook his head. "I better stick to water." She held it out a second longer, as if she expected him to change his mind. As she drew it back, she looked like she might say something, but let it drop.

She opened the second beer after returning the third and sat down next to Heaton. She pulled her gun from its holster, removed the clip, released the loaded bullet and kissed it before tucking it into her bra. Daniel glanced at Heaton, but he was guzzling his beer and had missed the action.

"Why do you do that?" he asked, concentrating on his sandwich preparation. He only glanced up to let her know he was talking to her.

"I don't like keeping a loaded gun in the house."

"Yeah, but why do you kiss the bullet? Is it a good luck thing?" He topped the three sandwiches with bread and grabbed plates from the cupboard. When she didn't answer, he looked over at her. She was watching him like he was a television chef worthy of teaching her something. He plated the uber-sandwiches and took them over. "I was just curious. You don't have to tell me." He added when he realized her reticence might have been because it was personal.

She twisted her beer on the counter, contemplating telling him. "I do it when I've had a bullet in the chamber. I don't like to pre-load my gun. It offers room for error. I only cock my gun when I suspect I might have to use it." Daniel and Heaton waited for her to fiddle with her plate before continuing. "If I load the bullet and I don't have to use it, then that's a good thing. I kiss it in thanks and place it next to my heart." She shrugged. "Nobody really wants to shoot if they don't have to."

Daniel cleared his throat. "So, you thank the bullet?" he asked tepidly.

Heaton reached over and flicked his ear. He yelped and looked at him in question of the assault. "She thanks God, you twit."

"Oh, right." Daniel caught her eye, but she looked away. She took a moment's pause before eating her sandwich. A quick silent prayer. Suddenly, the pieces of her contradictory behaviors made sense to him. Though his religious nature was only an afterthought in his life, for her, it was integral to knowing her motives.

He took a bite of his sandwich and glanced at Heaton. He must have sensed the epiphany, because he chomped down his sandwich and drank his beer in record time. When he was finished and had offered a healthy burp, he announced he needed to find Danato to fill him in, lest the paperwork for a bruised fem-wolf come through before he had a chance to explain the self-defense.

Daniel stared down at his half-eaten sandwich. It didn't hold the answers to anything, but it kept his eyes from wandering. He couldn't help but think about what Heaton had said. He wondered if his misery and conflicting feelings were just the ingredients to love. He wasn't sure he was capable of that. Even if he was, the list of differences between him and Nevia had just gotten even longer.

Then there was the small matter of last night, when he basically told her he never wanted to sleep with her again, which wasn't true, of course. He had been mad at her last night. This morning, he was mad at himself. Now coming around to the afternoon, he was right back where he started. He wanted her so badly he could hardly keep from grabbing her at any given moment. However, he resented her for trying to make him something he didn't want to be: a better person.

Somewhere in that twist of emotions, he found room to respect her as well. For a self-professed womanizer, that was new. He had never respected a woman he had slept with before, at least not after sleeping with them. It had nothing to do with the sex, but he put women into two categories: those willing to sleep with him and those not. He generally felt the women who didn't sleep with him to be the wiser of the two.

So perhaps it *was* about the sex.

Or he really was a sociopath.

Daniel looked at Nevia. She was chewing the last bit of her sandwich. She had hardly touched her beer. He really wanted to be that guy for her, but...

"I'm sorry I was such an arse last night," he blurted out when he found the courage to break the silence. She looked up at him, waiting for more. "Well, not just last night, but... always."

"You're not always an ass, Daniel," she said with her mouth partially full. She sipped on her beer to get the rest of her food down.

"You were right to push me. I really needed to heal Heaton. I owed him that and then some."

Nevia tipped her head. "Is that it, then? You've healed Heaton and now you can go back to normal."

Daniel sighed and pushed his sandwich away. He was hoping to avoid a fight, but apparently his apology just opened a door to more pestering.

"I'm sorry," she amended herself and tossed her hands up in surrender. "That's not fair. You can't decide your life based on my expectations. I'm pushing because I see what could be, but just because it *could* be doesn't mean it *needs* to be."

"Not everyone is cut out to be a superhero," he added.

She smiled and nodded. "I shouldn't have called you all those things. That was a low blow. I don't think of you like that."

"No, but it is how I think of myself, so maybe it was worth pointing out."

Nevia shook her head. "How do you come off so confident, even when you hate yourself so much?"

"Practice."

They fell into silence again and Nevia pushed off her stool.

"I'm going to head upstairs. Come get me if you need anything." Daniel tried not to think about what he needed from her. If she could smell his attraction, then she already knew. It was *want* by any definition, but it had grown into *need* when his fantasies started interfering with his life.

He wondered if it wasn't time to be bold again.

18

Daniel slipped through Nevia's open door. She was putting away her gun when she sensed him. She snapped up and looked at him like she was concerned he had come there to attack her. He shut the door and leaned against it so he had as much distance as possible between them, but he also made it clear that retreat was not an option.

"What is it, Daniel?" she asked, not hiding her irritation.

"Who was the religious fanatic? Your father or your mother?" he asked.

"What?" she asked, reaching for nothing in particular at her neckline.

"I'm just trying to put together your family history. Your grandfather was a werewolf. He had a half-breed daughter, your mother. I imagine your father didn't know about this until much later. He probably thought that by being an avid Christian, he might be able to keep the 'curse' from you."

Nevia took it all in, like the story he was telling was someone else's.

"It must have been hard growing up in your house. I'm sure the tattoo and the belly piercing were your way of rebelling. Your hair, your clothes, reflections of a disciplined life. I bet you joined the FBI just to spite him. He probably wanted you to be a teacher or something."

Daniel approached her. "I was just another rebellion. You probably worked hard in college, stayed out of trouble, but when it was all over and you had no prospects for a husband, the burden of waiting until you were married to experience sex probably seemed unreasonable."

Daniel stopped in front of her. He could see her breathing had increased. He was close enough to touch her, but he made sure he didn't. He wouldn't push that hard. He needed an invitation. "Am I on the right track?"

"My father found the piercing when I was seventeen. He misinterpreted it as a sexual lure. He threatened to cut off all my hair, to diminish my appeal and help me keep myself pure. I shaved my hair off the same day.

"They were both actually very proud of my career path. I got the tattoo in college. I did quite a few drugs in college, but yes, I focused on my studies. I didn't have any prospects for a husband, and after I got transferred here..."

"You figured you were even farther from that goal than before." He stepped closer to her. The space between them offered only enough room to stand. When she took in a deep breath, her breasts touched him. "Are you sure you're done rebelling with me?"

Her eyes flickered over his, and she swallowed hard. "I told you I'm not a one-night-stand kind of girl."

"I didn't stop this at one night. You did. I insisted on the second night. You know I've wanted you since this began."

"I can't be part of your harem."

"I have a history, but I don't have a harem. All I want is you."

"I know—the table, the couch, the bed."

"Yes, and your pushy encouragement, your drunken cockiness, your bad cooking, your great aim, your dead-on sniffer, your little prayers before you eat anything, and any other facet of your personality I haven't met yet. I want all that, in my bed, in my arms, and at my side."

"I don't believe you."

"Then read me deeper." Daniel opened his shirt for her to get a good whiff of whatever she needed to determine if he was deceiving her. He couldn't blame her for doubting him. His personality flaws had been served up on a platter since the day they met. The sudden change in menu must have really been throwing her for a loop.

She drew her face across his chest. Midway, she stopped and placed her forehead against his chest. "You have to understand, Daniel. I have no idea how to be in a relationship. You're the only man I've ever been with."

He leaned down and murmured in her ear. "Neither do I, but I'm pretty sure we can figure it out. As far as me being your only lover, I hope you don't mind, but I'm planning to keep it that way."

She looked up at him. Her fingers curled on his chest, clawing at him as she ran her hands down to his pants and undid them. All the while, she kept his eyes pinned with hers. As she reached within to jump start him, he grabbed the back of her neck and rested his forehead on hers. "I love that you aren't shy." Even as he said it, he could feel her trembling. "Aren't you going to kiss me?"

She looked up at him, like he had just asked her to do what she had already volunteered to do. She seemed more nervous about the kissing than the sex. He smiled and pulled her hand from his pants. "What do you say we start off at first base for a change?"

He sat down on her bed and pulled her into his lap. She looked everywhere but at him for a second. When she finally let him draw her into a kiss, she was tentative, like she was questioning if she was doing it right. Like all unpracticed kissers, with time, she loosened up and let her mouth explore his lips freely. Before long, she was trying to push him back to get more than his lips.

He resisted the temptation to repeat their past encounters and laid her down beneath him. Her body seemed even smaller beneath him. He pulled her top off and pinned her arms while he explored her breasts with his mouth. He wasn't one for bondage play, but this particular encounter was bringing out her claws, as it were.

He kissed down her stomach and released her to remove her pants. He was tempted to offer her another check mark on her sexual experiences, but he decided to save that for a special occasion, like a fine bottle of wine.

She frantically assisted him in removing his pants. He intentionally made her wait to slow down the experience. The first two times were over much too fast, even by a man's standards. He wanted more than a quick fix. He never wanted more than that, but this time he did. None of it made sense to him in his head, but everything about it made sense to his body.

By the time he took her, a gasp of pleasure and relief was shared between them. He wondered if she had been hoping for this despite her trepidations about being in a relationship with him.

Contrary to her shyness about kissing, she had no qualms about asking for what she wanted. He kept a slow rhythm, letting her beg for the speed that she thought she wanted. She had let him hang on her hook for three months without a release in sight. He didn't feel the least bit guilty about the pleasure he received from hearing her plead for him to alleviate *her* hunger.

Her hands grappled at him, demanding more. She dug her fingernails into his back and he made a mental note to clip them before round two. Finally obliging her request, he pushed her over the edge with ease, and he followed just behind her.

Panting against her, he almost wanted to cry. It was a strange feeling, out of place and unwanted, but somehow he knew he really needed her, not just wanted her. He could feel himself shaking, as he endeavored not to be overcome with sentiment. Nevia touched his shoulder, either questioning his state of mind or simply willing him to dismount, but he didn't respond to either. Instead, he pushed against her short and quick, sending her already primed body into another climax.

When he had calmed enough to look at her, he found the same impending doom mirrored in her eyes. In another twenty minutes, he would have her again, and maybe even twenty minutes after that, but it wouldn't be enough. He wouldn't tire of her, and somewhere in the middle of the afternoon, wet with sex, she would give up fighting her attraction to him and give herself to him completely. That offering alone scared the crap out of him, because he knew it meant that he would offer himself right back. They would be in a relationship.

They were so screwed.

19

THE DAY HAD GONE by quickly. Cori could already see the dimming light outside the high windows. If she weren't currently being held against her will, she might have been heading home to make supper.

When she heard footsteps in the hall, she rejoiced, hoping Ethan had come by to update her and give her a goodnight kiss before heading home himself. Her disappointment could not have been higher when she reached the door and found Leona approaching.

"Leona," she said with her mixed feelings bleeding into her voice.

"Cori," she said with a wink as she approached. She was alone. Her children were no doubt with their auntie Frederique or one of the other fem-wolves.

The guards blocked her approach and informed her she was too late for their preferred visiting hours. Cori shrank back, thinking that Ethan may not be down to see her after all.

Leona smiled demurely at the guards. "Oh merde, surely you could make an exception for me." She batted her eyes at the men. If she didn't have spit-up on her left shoulder and a fish cracker in her hair, they might have been prone to keel to her flirtation, but as she was, one of the guards wrinkled his nose at her, while the other shook his head.

"She's a fem-wolf, you idiots," Cori said, exasperated. "Just move or she'll rip your heads off." Cori thought that would be enough to make the men understand the gravity of what they faced, but apparently Clark's men didn't keep up on werewolf protocols.

"Oh, really," Idiot One said, approaching her. "I've heard a lot about fem-wolves."

"What did you hear?" Leona's French accent came out strong.

"I heard they're good in bed," he said huskily.

Cori couldn't help but sigh as she leaned against the side wall to watch what was probably going to be the most exciting part of her night. Too bad she didn't have popcorn.

"We are animals in the bedroom," Leona offered.

"Yeah," Idiot One drawled, "What do you say you and I slip into a cell down the way and you can prove it to me?"

"Actually," Cori called out, "can you just start right here? I'd really like to see her rip your tongue out when you try to kiss her."

"Shut up!" Idiot Two smacked the bars with his gun. Cori resisted the urge to see if she could duplicate her experience with Clark and freeze his hands to his gun.

Idiot One caressed Leona's cheek. Cori chortled at his stupidity. Idiot Two gave her a stern look, but it only made her laugh more.

"Did you hear anything else about fem-wolves?" Leona asked.

"Like what?" Idiot One said as he leaned in to kiss her neck.

"Did you hear that we don't screw men below our intelligence level?"

Idiot One's head flew back, and he glared aghast at Leona. "You bitch!" He shoved her back, and she moved back with the push, but Cori suspected she was playing the part of a lightweight human female just a little longer. "Get out of here!"

"No." Her flirtatious smile faded as if she was suddenly bored with the game. "*You* get out of here. I want to speak with my *friend.*" Cori could hear the way she said friend. The label repulsed her. Had it not been for Nevia, she might have missed the subtle inflection.

"I said get out of here!" Idiot One went back at her and shoved her, or at least tried to shove her. His feet slipped back as he pressed against her body, like he was trying to push a tree while wearing roller skates. He regained his balance, but none of his composure. Leona eyed him with curiosity, like she was drinking up his illumination. "What the hell are you?"

"What part of female werewolf don't you get?" Cori yelled from the cheap seats.

Idiot One didn't fully turn around to glare at her, but only because he didn't want to take his eyes off Leona. She walked toward him, but he pulled his rifle and aimed it at her. "Stay where you are or I'll shoot."

"Just shoot," Cori said. "It will speed things along."

Leona leaned around Idiot One to look at her. "Thank you for the vote of confidence, darling, but it does sting like the devil to get shot."

Cori grimaced. She hadn't really thought about the bruising impact a bullet might have on a fem-wolf—like getting punched with a very strong, very tiny fist. "Sorry."

Leona ducked back behind Idiot One just in time for his attempt to thrust the butt of his gun in her face. She blocked him and tossed him... across the entire section. Cori whistled and clapped as Idiot One flew. "Home run, Leona!"

"Are you quite enjoying yourself, Cori?" Leona scolded. Cori was going to make a comment about not having cable, but Idiot Two shot at Leona and interrupted the banter. Despite the suggestion of pain to bullets, Leona had virtually no recovery time before she leaped onto Idiot Two and ripped his gun out of his hand. She tossed the gun behind her and growled with hidden vocal depth. "I'm not supposed to kill humans. Don't make me break my streak."

Idiot Two flew across the room with just as much ease as Idiot One. He landed near his partner with the same *thunk* that encouraged unconscious meditation. Leona smoothed out her clothing before raising her gaze to Cori. The smile she held for her seemed so obviously forced to her now. She wondered if that was all due to Nevia's enlightenment, or if Cleos's blocker was keeping her instincts on track.

"Cori, my pet," Leona began.

"I'm not your pet," Cori snapped before she had cause to.

Leona sloughed off the indignation. "I thought I smelled you around here when I came in for the trial."

"Oh yeah, how's that going?" Cori pretended to be interested to keep the conversation off of her current predicament.

Leona smiled for real. "Very well," she said, linking her hands through the bars to touch Cori's hands. Cori tried not to flinch at her touch, but she found the woman more threatening without her hypnotic abilities. "Aren't you going to share with me your woes?" Leona's eyes circled the room within.

"You mean the cage?" Cori looked around as if she was noticing it for the first time as well. "Oh, you know me. I like to push the envelope."

"Yes, you do push people's buttons." Cori could see a sparkle of honest amusement in her eyes. "Whose buttons did you push this time?"

Cori wondered if there was any reason not to tell her about the incident, but since she didn't want to outright sever their semi-friendly interaction, she opted to continue the conversation civilly. "I helped three prisoners escape and pissed off... everyone."

Leona laughed. "You really are fearless, aren't you?"

Cori shook her head. "No, I just don't always think before I leap."

"What do you say we get you out of here?" Before Cori could respond, Leona ripped the door to the cell open, breaking the formerly solid iron lock. Considering it was designed to withstand the strength of a male werewolf; it was no small feat. Cori suspected it was less a gesture of generosity and more a display of her strength.

The lack of bars between them made her more concerned than she was prepared for. The time it took her to respond made her fear that the block on her psyche hadn't worked.

"Well?" Leona asked again.

"Well, what? I can't leave. Danato hasn't given me permission to."

Leona stepped close to her. Cori closed her eyes and took in the suffocating scent of perfume and werewolf musk. "Let's not worry about Danato right now. Let's just take a walk."

Cori could feel the pressure of Leona's words begging her to do what she was asking, but unlike before, she didn't feel petrified with fear. Leona leaned in to kiss her, but Cori turned her head to avoid her petroleum-based lipstick. "Seriously, Leona, I am *so* not into the girl-on-girl stuff. Do you mind if we keep this a little less friendly?"

Cori had expected Leona to be annoyed by her lack of control. What she didn't expect was the shock on her face, and the utter disappointment that followed. "What is this?" She looked over her eyes for the familiar glaze that her seduction usually inspired. "What did you do?" she seethed with undue repulsion.

"I got a mental block so you can't hypnotize me," Cori answered, taking a step back to alleviate her sinuses from the assaulting perfume.

"Who told you I was hypnotizing you?" she asked with eyes narrowed.

"Jordan told me you and—"

"That mixed-breed stuck her nose in my business!"

Cori instantly regretted releasing her informant's identity. She didn't suspect that Leona would even remember her.

"I would have found out eventually," Cori lied, hoping to detract from Jordan's blame.

"You wouldn't have figured it out! You're as much a simpleton as those two." Leona tossed her head toward the two guards, who were passed out on the other side of the section.

"I am not a simpleton!" Cori knew she was playing with fire to start a shouting match with Leona, but the truth was she was still kind of irked that Leona didn't respect her like she thought she did.

"You think because you have a slightly more informed view of the world than the rest of the human race that you are smart? You're just a well-trained rat in a maze!"

"Yeah, well, this rat bested your ass!" That fire she was just playing with suddenly turned into a forest fire.

"Bested me!" Leona stuttered as she came at her full-force. Cori put up her hands in self-defense and hoped against hope that Leona still didn't want to break her streak.

When Leona grabbed her throat, she felt her feet lift like she was a rag doll. She squeezed her throat tight, but Cori could still breathe—sort of. She grappled with her arms, but resisted the urge to claw into her skin, since she knew it wouldn't do any good. "Leona," she choked before she could apologize.

"You never bested me! You got in a lucky shot! You are nothing but a plaything to me."

Cori didn't have many female friends, maybe none, unless it wasn't too soon to count Jordan as one. Leona had been a woman she admired for her strength and confidence. She was someone Cori thought she could have gotten along with if it hadn't been for Vince. Hearing her express her true opinion of her wasn't nearly as painful as she expected, but it did make her angry.

Cori wanted to say several choice words to her, starting at the high spectrum of profanity and ending with words irreconcilable with the English language. However, since her neck was currently in a visc, she settled for a stress relieving scream that would at least be an objection to her treatment.

Cori could feel the temperature rise as she closed her eyes, but she ignored it. Her scream came out low and muffled until Leona's grip released. She opened her eyes as she fell back to the ground. Leona's body flew out of the cell, ushered by a fireball spreading across her chest.

Cori had just enough time to get in one choice high-spectrum cuss before the fem-wolf landed.

20

E THAN HEARD CORI SCREAM as he entered the section. He ran to her rescue, but her attacker was nowhere near her. Leona was lying on the floor, stunned by something. Her eyes were beyond maniacal. She stood up and dusted off her singed clothing while she eyed Cori. She seemed leery of approaching Cori and kept her distance.

Leona looked like she might cry, but since she wasn't a weak-willed woman, Ethan knew better than to see her emotional break as anything less than dangerous. He hung back to observe and waited for her to make her next move.

At the moment that any other woman might have burst into tears, Leona's face cleared of sentiment, and a smile returned—a warning for the events to follow. Ethan took a few steps forward in case she actually attacked, but as he suspected, Leona wasn't planning a physical attack. Leona wanted to wound Cori a different way.

21

CORI WAS GLAD THAT she hadn't killed Leona, but part of her had hoped that she would be a little more hurt. Leona was up and moving again in less than a minute, which didn't bode well for Cori since she didn't know if she could keep up her defense. She barely understood the electricity she randomly threw out, let alone this new fireball trick.

Leona looked miserable with the realization that Cori could actually defend herself. She had always viewed Cori as beneath her. Between the colloidal silver incident, Ethan's loyalty to her, and now this. She must have been having a hard time coddling her ego.

Just when Cori thought Leona might completely break down, an epiphany seemed to form in her wicked little mind. She smiled, but didn't advance. She waited outside the door, watching her, as if she wanted to memorize the moment. Her head dipped, letting her eyes glower at her beneath the ridge of her brow. "I fucked him, you know," Leona purred.

Cori felt her body go numb, and her defensive stance fell away. She felt sick to her stomach. "What?"

"Your man. I fucked him every chance I got. He didn't want to, but he didn't complain after it was all said and done."

Cori wanted to puke. She wasn't sure if it was the hyperventilating or the stinging heat wave taking over her body that was making her lightheaded, but she thought she might pass out soon. "No... he said..."

"He told you what you needed to hear. He gave you your clear conscience so you could go on just as before."

"That's enough, Leona!" Ethan came into view from the hall. When he turned to face Cori, she crumpled into the corner of her cell and shook her head at him. She couldn't believe he had lied to her.

22

ETHAN COULD HEAR CORI'S heavy breathing. She was either about to cry or about to pass out. It surprised him she was taking the news so hard. He would have thought that her feelings for Vince would have dimmed enough that she wouldn't have felt anything more than disappointment at a corrupted memory.

When she offered her objection to Leona's admission, Ethan knew instantly that she was assuming Leona meant him. Since Leona hadn't specifically said Vince's name, Cori naturally thought of Ethan. Leona had no idea that she was torturing her with the wrong man.

"That's enough, Leona!" Ethan intervened before it could go any further. Leona didn't seem surprised by his presence, which meant she was enjoying the audience he provided for his wife's torture. She glared at him for the interruption, but smiled when she saw the effect it had on him.

He turned to Cori and approached her recoiled, cornered body. She shook her head, releasing the tears she had been trying to hold onto so she didn't add to Leona's triumph. She tried to speak, but a sob choked out her efforts.

"Cori, not me, Vince." He stayed at the door, blocking her view of Leona. She kept her eyes trained on him. The realization of what he was saying was dawning, but she didn't give up her hold on her pain, in case she was misinterpreting him. "Leona slept with Vince after your encounter. She did it just to spite you, and to prove to him that she could win. He kept it from you, to protect you. He knew you would be devastated by his involuntary philandering."

"Don't pander to her, it was more than voluntary," Leona barked over his shoulder.

"Shut *up*, Leona!" he barked right back, barely offering her a glance. "I'm sorry, Cori," he offered. "I didn't tell you because I didn't think it was something you ever needed to know. I should have known she would use it against you eventually."

Cori recovered from her near panic attack and stood up, wiping her eyes. "You didn't sleep with her?"

"No Cori, I was telling you the truth." Ethan could sense Leona's approach, but he didn't react like she wanted him to. She wrapped her arms around his chest and lowered one hand to his crotch. Cori glared at the groping, but she didn't advance.

"We gave it a go, though, didn't we?" Leona said, sneering around him at Cori.

"Cori," Ethan drew her eyes back to him. He didn't bother shaking off Leona, he was happy to prove to her once again how little effect she had on his body. "Before I left to help Leona, I asked Mezula for some help."

Cori's face crumpled at the sound of Mezula being involved, but she didn't interrupt. Her eyes trailed again to Leona's hands on him. She was getting angry that he wasn't fending her off, so he sped up his explanation. "She gave me control of my body. Leona can threaten to force herself on me, but unless I want it, she can't. Isn't that right, Leona?" Ethan looked over at Leona, who was biting his arm playfully.

She looked at him with a livid stare. He was ruining her fun.

"Getting anything down there?" Ethan nodded down to her fruitless search. She ripped her hand away and shoved him into the door frame. It was enough of a push to make him think twice about reacting to it, but not enough to knock the wind out of him.

Ethan moved to Cori. She was still figuring out how to react to everything.

"Leona tried to seduce me. She tried to force me, just like you feared she would, but I had planned ahead for that." He glanced back at Leona, who was losing control of her will not to cry. "This is done, Leona. You can't hurt her anymore. Vince's deception only proves his devotion to her." Ethan gripped Cori's shoulders so she would know she should take that to heart. It felt weird to hear him defending a man he had resented so much, but he didn't want Cori's image of him to be sullied. "She can still keep her memory of a man who was willing to do anything to protect their love."

Cori's eyes flickered over his. She hadn't said anything for a while, and he hoped that meant that she was coming to terms with everything, and not bottling up her reactions.

"You are both pathetic!" Leona hissed.

Ethan looked back at Leona, but didn't move from Cori. "What bothers you more, Leona? That you can't break our love, or that we *have* love to begin with?"

Leona turned and stomped away. Ethan knew she didn't want them to see that she was crying. He knew she had feelings for Callin that she wouldn't allow herself to indulge in. Lord knows what he saw in her, but any love separated by political boundaries and taboos was likely to break even the hardest of hearts—even a fem-wolf's.

Ethan turned his attention back to Cori. He had expected to console her a little more about the loss of her idealistic image of Vince, but she kissed him hard. Her hands reached under his arms and latched onto his shoulders. She climbed him like a tree, wrapping her legs around his waist.

He felt the need to further explain why he'd decided to defend himself against Leona. He also felt he should apologize for not breaking the news about Vince to her himself, so she could have avoided this attack from Leona, but she seemed to have already forgiven him.

There were a million more things to discuss about her incarceration, but it wasn't words she needed and he was more than happy to satisfy her needs.

Ethan pushed her back into the corner. He considered putting her on the cot, but he was aware of which cell they were in, and he didn't want to overlap any old memories. It wasn't a competition. Vince was important to her, but he was part of her memories. She belonged to Ethan now, and he most definitely belonged to her.

He unfurled her legs from his back, just long enough to slip her out of her jeans. Her urgency didn't offer him the option of fully disrobing, but since this was an unauthorized conjugal visit, he wasn't sure they had time for all that.

He wondered what had excited Cori more: his devotion to keep true to her, or that she was now the only woman permitted to wake his desire. Either way, he was happy to feel her against him.

Ethan pushed up against her, firm and frenzied, to give her what she wanted. She buried her teeth in his shoulder to muffle her enthusiasm. The tinge of pain ushered him to the end with her. When she was satiated and her body relaxed, she draped against him, and for a moment he just held her, understanding how much the last 24 hours had taken out of her.

He released her so she could stand, but stayed next to her to balance her. He slipped his pants back up and helped her with hers, since she was still whirling in the post-coital rush.

"Please forgive me," Cori whispered in his ear as he got her free leg back into her jeans. He pulled her pants up and looked at her. She was crying. It wasn't an unusual sight, but the grief in her eyes reminded him of their last major blowout, save the baby argument. "I'm so sorry. I didn't mean to screw everything up."

Any anger he might have had about her betrayal had been dismissed in the heat of passion. Cori was Cori. She was always getting into trouble. She was always making bad choices that amazingly resulted in good outcomes. He loved her for her, and a little thing like *un*-escaped prisoners and an unmentioned key couldn't change that.

"When I saw Clark shoot Hirem, it was like he shot you. It was like watching you die." She sniffled uncontrollably.

Ethan didn't understand the association, but he understood the pain. He pulled her into a hug. "I forgive you, Cori." He pulled her away, even though she wasn't ready to release the embrace. Ethan pulled a thread of hair away from her eyes. "Cori, you're never going to do anything to break my love. You might disappoint me or make me mad or even make me sad, but it's you and me all the way. You just got to try a little harder at keeping me updated as things come along, okay?"

She nodded and her eyes widened. "Efrat kissed me again. I didn't want him to, but I'm pretty sure he won't do it again." She threw the words at him as if he might not be able to get mad if they were bandage-ripping quick. "I went to see Cleos without telling you yesterday to get a mental block against the fem-wolves, and I got scratched up by the vampires by accident."

Ethan's eyes widened with concern, but she kept going, throwing the facts at him quicker than he could comprehend. "I was afraid to tell you, so I asked Daniel to heal me, and he promised not to tell you because he didn't want us to have an argument and break up over something so stupid. It doesn't even matter now, because Cleos hates me. My rings went bat-shit crazy on him. And I'm not sure I'm ready to have a baby, but I love you so much and I don't want you to be mad at me."

"Okay, okay." Ethan pulled her into another hug and rubbed her back. "I hear you. I hear you." He pulled her over to the cot and sat her down so he could look at her. She whimpered and looked away. "No, no, no, look at me." He pulled her face back.

"I think you've been building up for a breakdown, and little Miss Mutt was your last straw. First off, you've been working way too hard. When we get you out of here—and we *will* get you out of here—I'm going to have a long discussion with Belus about union-approved working hours. Next, thank you for telling me about... everything. You may have to give me the footnotes on those confessions later. Third, don't worry about the baby thing. I am happy. Nothing needs to change. I just had a picture in my mind, that's all.

"And finally, I believe you mentioned something about us 'breaking up'." He air-quoted the phrase. "Sweetness, this is marriage. We don't get to break up. The only option is the D-word, and believe me, that is never happening. I fought long and hard to get you and I am keeping you. So, buckle up for the long haul, because there isn't a restraining order, fem-wolf, or circumstance that could keep me away from you."

Her eyes flickered over his, and he recognized the awe inspired by his devotion to her. He smiled as she unconsciously licked her lips. "You're going to attack me again, aren't you?"

She didn't bother responding. She just straddled him and kissed him hard, like she had minutes earlier. He laughed at her vigor as he carried her back to the corner. He afforded a glance outside to make sure the minions were still passed out.

This time he turned her around, so neither of them had to dispatch too much clothing in case they were interrupted. He knew indulging their appetites during such a precarious situation was inappropriate, but he also knew Cori needed to relieve some stress, and so did he.

23

D ANATO WASN'T SURE WHAT Efrat had meant about Cori having episodes, but he agreed with his concerns regarding Clark. He wasn't sure what happened up there last night, but Cori had hinted at feeling personally assaulted by Hirem's death. Her animosity toward Clark was warranted, but he wasn't sure he had ever heard her actually wish someone dead, with the exception of Efrat. And even that hadn't lasted.

He was certain that there was still something missing from Cori's story, but he didn't have the energy to investigate it properly. He was already missing an entire night of sleep, so he had no guilt about leaving Heaton to fill Belus in on the fem-wolf situation. He knew from Heaton's presence that things hadn't gone as planned, but as long as no one was dead, he didn't really care.

By the time he made it to the house, he remembered Cori wasn't going to be home to make dinner, and since Ethan was likely to spend the remainder of the evening with her, he would need to make dinner for the crew himself.

When he walked in to find Daniel and Nevia behind his stove, and the smell of sizzling onions wafting through the house, he let out a sigh of relief. He caught the tail end of an argument about whether or not to add the rest of the vegetables into the pan with the onions, or fry them separately.

"Where did you learn to cook?" Daniel said. "Everybody knows you fry all the veggies separately."

Nevia scoffed at his perfectionism. "No one does that. It's ratatouille. Just throw it in a pan and cook it until the crunch is gone."

"Give me that spoon." Daniel ripped the wooden spoon from her hand and pretended to swat her with it before he was interrupted by the front door shutting.

Danato nodded to the two faces that were equally surprised and embarrassed to see him. "I wasn't aware that you cooked, Daniel," he said after hanging up his coat.

Daniel cleared his throat and shrugged. "It's not my best talent, but I haven't killed any taste buds yet." Daniel shifted uncomfortably when Danato didn't laugh. "That was just a joke."

Danato nodded. "I know, Daniel." Danato offered him a small smile. "I'm just a little tired. Thank you for starting dinner and... for taking care of the trial."

Daniel looked like a deer in headlights, but he recovered enough to pull Nevia's hand away from the skillet to keep her from adding the next vegetable. "I... ah... the fem-wolf was attacking. I didn't intend to..."

"I don't even want to know tonight." Daniel's attempt at an explanation impressed Danato. He was usually closed-mouthed when he thought he had done something wrong. He imagined that change in his personality was due to the introduction of Nevia.

"Jordan," Danato said with unconcealed exhaustion in his voice, "would you mind joining me in my office?"

She gave him a hint of a nod and came around the counter. Daniel caught her arm. She looked at him for the answer, but Daniel was already looking at Danato. "Anything you have to say about me, you can say *to* me, Danato. I can handle it."

Danato exchanged a glance with Nevia before responding. "I'm glad to hear it, Daniel, but this isn't about you."

Nevia waited for Daniel to release her before she continued around the island. Danato gave her the lead to the office. He glanced back at Daniel before he left, but his eyes were back on the skillet.

Nevia sat down in one of the chairs in front of his desk, while he took his main desk chair. He had many times brought Ethan or Cori into this room to disarm them when he needed to be the disciplinarian. Never before had he felt disarmed himself, until now. Even sitting in his dominant chair with a gigantic desk between them, he felt exposed before this woman.

He shifted uncomfortably, trying to decide how to approach the subject he needed but didn't want to discuss.

"This afternoon…" he began, but didn't continue. He half expected Nevia to jump in, but she waited patiently for him to gather his thoughts. "I hadn't taken into consideration how much insight you might have into my life," he finally managed to say.

Nevia nodded. "I haven't told anyone about your… condition."

Danato sighed in relief. "Good, good. I hope that it won't be too much trouble to keep it that way. Belus is the only one who knows about my little hitchhikers."

"I'm pretty good at keeping secrets, but I'll tell you the same thing that I told my last secret-holder." Nevia paused, either for effect or to offer him the opportunity to dispel her opinion. "Secrets eventually surface and usually at the most inopportune time. So, be prepared for the consequences of holding onto them too long."

"I've already suffered the consequences." Danato raised his cane.

"I'm no one to you, but if you want my opinion, I'll give it." Nevia paused and waited for his permission to continue. Danato raised his brow and nodded. "Ethan and Cori love you, and you love them. You should open yourself up to them."

Danato furrowed his brow. "That's it?" He had expected a lot more: a scathing retribution for his deceit, or perhaps a poetic proverb.

She stood up and headed to the door. She stopped with the doorknob in hand and looked back at him. "Isn't that enough?"

She left, shutting the door behind her. It wasn't a scathing retribution, but it served the same purpose.

24

"R ATATOUILLE!" Heaton scoffed at Daniel as he took the casserole out of the oven. "Who the hell eats that?"

"You do, you twat. The fridge was overflowing with vegetables from Cori's gardening." Daniel threw the potholders at him. They smacked him in the face, and Heaton retorted with a playful slap on the cheek. "Ohhhh! Now it's on, you cheeky English bastard."

Daniel and Heaton mock wrestled until they heard Danato harrumph from his chair in the living room. They both released their grips and went back to their corners. Heaton grabbed a piece of the casserole and tasted it. He shrugged, a vague consensus on its palatability.

"Where's Ethan, anyway?" Daniel asked.

Heaton tipped his eyebrow. "Saying goodnight to Cori."

Daniel scoffed. "Yeah, right, I don't think the general would allow that."

"How're things here?" Heaton offered another tip of his eyebrow along with a nod at Nevia, who was sitting on the couch reading.

Daniel smiled, but covered it quickly. "Fine."

Heaton grinned at him relentlessly. "You're such a child." He reached for another nibble of the casserole and Daniel smacked his hand.

"Speaking of." Daniel looked over at Danato and leaned in a little closer to conceal the conversation from him. "Danato and Nevia had a little talk earlier."

Heaton leaned in as well. "What about?"

"I don't know. She won't tell me. Says it's not her secret to tell."

"Really?" Heaton's brow furrowed.

"Yeah, that's the second time I've heard that from her. Apparently, she has the burden of keeping *two* secrets from me."

Heaton's face dawned with the insinuation. He drew in a breath like he was about to explain something, but Danato interrupted. "You boys have something to share, or were you thinking that gossip wasn't just for twelve-year-old girls?"

Heaton and Daniel perked up and looked at Danato before exchanging a look. "We were just commenting on how many secrets there are running around this house," Daniel said, coming around the island. He looked at Heaton to back him up. Heaton rolled his eyes and rounded the other side of the island, but he didn't offer any backup.

"There are indeed," Danato commented with suspicion in his voice.

Daniel stood between the couch and Danato's chair with his arms akimbo. Danato stared at him with a sort of amusement in his eyes.

"For example," Daniel started. Heaton groaned. Nevia shook her head at him. Danato raised his chin, no doubt hoping for an excuse to throw him into a wall. "What is the secret to getting this house to switch décor?" Daniel pointed to the dead animal hanging above the fireplace.

Danato actually laughed at his ill-timed joke, which wasn't entirely a joke. The house had the same décor every time he had been in it, which wasn't often, but over the span of a half-decade, it seemed to lack the subtle updates one might expect.

"I wasn't aware that my furnishings offended you," Danato said.

"They don't offend, but the spare bedrooms offer more variety than this room, and they only have three furnishings and one wall-hanging."

Danato smiled, and for a moment Daniel thought he might have just been placating him, waiting for the best time to surrender to his urge to yell at him, but he didn't. "I sure do like it when you boys come to visit. Makes me appreciate Ethan and Cori's bickering a lot more."

Daniel tipped his head at Danato. He looked back at Heaton to confirm it. Heaton shrugged and snickered. "Was that a jibe?" he asked Heaton. "I think I just got slammed, and it wasn't my head."

"That could be arranged, if you're disappointed." Danato donned another smile, letting him know he was kidding.

"Wow, two in a row," Daniel reveled as Ethan came in. "I think I'll stop while I'm ahead." Daniel greeted Ethan with raised arms. "At last, we can eat."

"I hope you didn't wait on my account," Ethan said, smelling the air.

"Well, we weren't sure you'd make it home." Daniel winked as he brought the casserole to the table.

Ethan sat down and Heaton settled in beside him, while Daniel took a seat across from them. "How is she?" Heaton asked as Danato sat down. He looked just as interested in the answer.

Nevia sat at the far end of the table. Daniel made it a point to push out the chair beside him, but she seemed content to sit away from him. He wasn't sure if she wanted to keep her distance, or was just used to sitting away from everyone, but either way, he didn't like it. Not after making so much progress to get close to her that afternoon.

"She's more stressed out than I anticipated. She had an incident with Leona."

"Leona?" Danato nearly choked on his first bite. "Is she alright?"

"Yeah, apparently she got a mental block to keep Leona from hypnotizing her."

Daniel looked up when he heard mental block mentioned. Ethan gave him a small glare. "Yeah, I know you healed her."

Daniel frowned and shoved a finger at Nevia. "She made me do it."

"Nice pluck, dude," Heaton chided him.

"Fuck pluck, he won't hit *her*," Daniel complained.

"I did make him do it," Nevia defended him. "I was also the one who advised Cori to get the block. She wouldn't have even been down there if it weren't for me."

"Down where?" Danato chimed in, sounding offended that he had to ask.

"The basement," Ethan said. "She went to see Cleos."

"Cleos," Danato balked. "I thought we were done with that."

"We are," Ethan clarified slowly, and he attempted to enjoy his food.

"Clearly not, if Cleos is messing around in her head again," Danato snarled.

"Cori needed the block," Nevia intervened. "She is one of the lucky few that are prone to being hypnotized by fem-wolves."

"Hypnotized?" Danato balked again. "I've never heard of that."

"That doesn't negate it as a truth. She took my advice. I take full responsibility for not accompanying her, but I was under the assumption that Cori was a grown adult."

Daniel grimaced as Danato bristled at Nevia's condescension. Heaton did his best to hide his smile.

"She is, but she is an employee and I expect to be informed of her activities," Danato growled.

"Frankly, this is what I was referring to earlier, Danato. You have such high expectations of translucency for your employees, but you don't offer that in return."

Daniel could see Ethan join the ranks of the shocked. Heaton lost his smile when Danato's napkin slapped down onto the table.

"That's enough," Danato threatened, but the storm belying his controlled voice didn't seem to affect Nevia.

"From what I gather of the situation, Cori saw a problem, and she fixed it. The only issue that is causing so much condescending examination is the fact that she did it without your express permission."

Danato's chest puffed. "I am her boss."

"Hardly. You live in the same house as her. You express your love through exaggerated protectiveness. I assure you, Danato, she views you as a father. Take it from someone who knows, that kind of love can have its limits."

"I appreciate your insight, Jordan, but I don't—"

"There is no need to placate me, Danato. It doesn't work. I know you're pissed about having a newcomer telling you your business, but I can't help it. Cori doesn't need you to keep saving her. She needs you to back her up. That's how you'll get her trust and translucency, which is how you'll keep her safe. I back up my partners, and they back me up. That's how we get our job done and stay alive. I know I'm just a lowly hunter and not the warden of an entire prison, but I think that particular system might also be effective here."

Everyone stared down at their plates, trying to slowly inch themselves down in their chairs until they disappeared under the table. Nevia finished her rant with a perturbed huff, like she was just as frustrated at having to say it as Danato was to hear it. She dug into her food without regard to the steely glare coming from across the table.

Danato stayed poised for a verbal counterattack, but eventually he sobered and placed his napkin back in his lap. "How does the mental block work?" he asked, taking a bite of his food.

Nevia nodded as she finished chewing her food so she could swallow before speaking. She delicately dabbed the corners of her mouth with her napkin. Daniel couldn't help but be amused since she was usually the first among them to let out a rumbling burp when they were drinking.

"The brain contains a section that is designed to allow psychic activity. On supernatural beings, this area is hyperactive. On regular beings it's only slightly active, but it is susceptible to hypnotic suggestion from beings of higher psychic activity. A mental block is designed to dampen outside influences."

Daniel glanced at Ethan and Heaton, who were shocked by the sudden change in conversation. They started to eat once again, and the discomfort washed away with Nevia's description.

"It won't prevent psychic readings, but it should keep her safe from your lesser seducers. I would actually advise all of you to have it done. Even though you're immune to fem-wolves, it could help you keep a mental standing if you had to interact with a seducer."

Daniel smiled as she continued to educate Danato. She caught his eye once or twice, but she didn't offer him the smile that his now love-sick ego desperately wanted. He was so screwed.

25

T HE NEXT MORNING, DANIEL could feel eyes on him as he entered the area designated for Callin's trial. He wasn't sure what he expected to encounter. Sideways glances with ire and murderous intent would have been his first guess. Dodging fisticuffs would have been his second guess. Instead, the council hushed at his entrance and marked it with silent observation.

The glares he anticipated were replaced by probing assessments. He didn't feel threatened, but rather stripped naked. It was the same freakish fascination Nevia held for him. He didn't want to delve too deeply into the relationship between these women and Nevia, but it was a notable similarity.

Frederique nodded to him respectfully. It was the same nod he might have given a man he had brawled with the night before. It was an acknowledgement of the battle—won or lost—and a peace offering at the same time.

Her eyes moved behind him to Nevia. She was following behind him some distance back. He hadn't spent the night with her last night, even though he wanted to. It was too early in their relationship for him to make assumptions about his territories and privileges. He only hoped that her intentional distance was for the sake of professionalism and not a backslide in their progress.

Nevia had veered off course and met up with Leona. Overnight, the new mother had transformed. Her attempts at hair and makeup were reduced to barrettes and a smattering of face powder. Her expensive suit was now a pair of gray slacks and a loose top that was no doubt just as expensive as her suits, but looked business casual. She was plain and unassuming, but she looked rested, and was not dappled with baby vomit and food remnants.

Nevia gave her a wide berth and kept her movements slow. "Is she well?" she asked, motioning to the carrier holding the newborn girl. Daniel could just make out the cast wrapping her leg.

Leona stood up and Daniel froze, prepared for the impending altercation or sarcastic response that she had made herself known for. Instead, she nodded. "Yes," she said so meekly that he almost couldn't hear it. She couldn't hide her response from a room full of animal-inspired ears, so he assumed she was simply offering an apology with the decibel level. "She will heal without repercussions. The doctor said she is developing slower than average, but she is healthy."

"Good." Nevia looked down at the baby. "She is a beautiful child."

Leona nodded at the compliment. When Nevia turned to leave, Leona reached out to her. The sudden movement caused a moment of tension in Daniel's body, but the open hand resting on Nevia's shoulder was no more a threat than a verbal "excuse me." When Nevia turned, Leona waffled for a moment. She didn't seem to be the type to lack words, but she was without them for several seconds.

"Thank you," she finally said. It was either the only words she had, or a brief summation of the many words she couldn't express with any accuracy at the moment.

"You're welcome," Nevia said with a demure smile. She got back on course and saw Daniel watching her. Her annoyance gave him pause, and he pretended to look at something else before moving on to join Heaton and Ethan in the bleachers.

Nevia didn't like being babysat. Most women claimed to be independent-minded and self-assured, but Nevia actually was. She was confident in her abilities, assertive in her opinions, and most importantly, she knew when to shut up. It sounded archaic and domineering, but women—at least the women Daniel was familiar with—spent too much time speaking about nothing. Not that women shouldn't speak, but better to make your statement and walk away than to batter your point until the objective is blurred into disinterest.

Daniel gave Heaton a grimace as he climbed the bleachers. Heaton laughed at him. "In trouble already?"

"Aye, I guess that was my warning to mind my own business." He settled down in the ample space between Heaton and Ethan. They had probably left the space there to keep the chumminess at a palatable level, but he didn't want to lean over to talk across, so he took it for a saved seat. They adjusted appropriately while he slumped down and did his best to pretend Nevia didn't exist. It was a fruitless attempt since she was already *actually* ignoring him.

"I'm surprised Leona is being civil," Ethan said, looking over at her. "She looks almost normal. I barely see the 'elitist French bitch' tattooed across her forehead."

Heaton and Daniel chuckled at that.

"What is your main objection to her?" Heaton asked.

"It's a long story and most of it isn't mine, but the most recent event happened last night when she tried to hurt Cori."

Daniel whipped his head over. "Hurt?"

Heaton nudged him. "Easy, Daniel, let him finish."

"Emotionally hurt. We handled it." Ethan looked lost in thought for a moment. "I think the entire incident finally broke her, though."

"Cori?" Heaton asked.

"No, Leona. She hit rock bottom last night, you know. Her favorite chew toy is biting back." Ethan sighed like just the memory of it was tiresome. "I don't know what Callin sees in her." He nodded to Callin, who was admiring Leona and his child from his cell. Leona was at least returning his gaze. She even turned her baby boy so that

Callin could see his face. He lit up at the view of his child. "He deserves the right to be with his child," Ethan said with almost as much bitterness as Nevia might have.

"Yes, he does," Nevia chimed in from her spot below them. Daniel and Heaton exchanged a look of concern. Between Ethan and Nevia, the *unbiased observer* title was starting to crumble.

"I think we are all in agreement with that," Heaton said diplomatically, "but we are no more a part of this trial than a fan is a coach to a televised game. We need to remain impartial, or risk another incident like yesterday."

"That incident was caused by Frederique's unwillingness to listen to Callin," Nevia hissed, trying to keep her volume down while the council members questioned the father of Leona's baby girl.

"He was soapboxing. This isn't a political forum."

"Bullshit!" Nevia's volume passed the ignorable limits and several faces looked over. Daniel smiled and waved at them, offering a mouthed apology. Heaton nudged him again and nodded for him to say something.

Daniel's mouth dropped open, and he shrugged. Heaton didn't necessarily offer the option of saying no, so he begrudgingly slipped down beside Nevia. "Let's go for a walk," he mumbled.

"Not now," she answered distractedly.

Daniel glanced back at Heaton. He was starting to feel the complications of being in a relationship with his partner. He had always followed Heaton's lead, but since

Nevia had bullied her way into the alpha dog spot, she wasn't likely to listen to him. The only advantage he had was the boyfriend card. Since the card had yet to be laminated, he felt like a heel using it.

"Nevia, we need to speak privately." She turned to him and offered him a glare that he hadn't thought possible. He didn't imagine seeing her angry at him would hurt so much, but it did. He wanted to be the source of her joy, not her ire. At that moment, he questioned everything, just as he had two nights ago. If she hadn't softened at that moment, he would have walked away and given up any hope of being with her. He wasn't a proud man, but he certainly wouldn't be in a relationship with a woman that hated him. He had already seen his parents endure that. He wanted no part of it.

She either sensed his disappointment or read the depth of it on his face, because she calmed her attitude and agreed to leave with him. They shuffled off the bleachers and skirted behind them. Heaton watched him go with a stern expression that told him he wasn't to let her come back until she had calmed down.

It was way too early for him to be volleying his loyalties like this.

26

ANIEL FOLLOWED NEVIA INTO the next section. It was the same line of cells as the last section, minus the tenants and the trial. She turned around and crossed her arms, waiting for him to speak. The ever-present holstered gun only exaggerated her "Don't fuck with me" image. She would have been scary if she wasn't so damned cute.

"What, Daniel?" she asked.

"What's going on, Nevia? You're usually cool as a cucumber."

"Do you realize how important this trial is?"

"No, explain it to me," he said honestly, wanting to understand.

"Callin is the first werewolf to make a stand against the council. He isn't just demanding that he have rights to his children, he's demanding that *all* males have rights to their children."

"Okay, so let's help him do that by staying calm."

"They won't approve it. This trial is a joke."

"Joke or not, it has to happen so they can appear to give a damn, so let Callin say his piece and he can go from there. He won't be in jail indefinitely. He can continue this fight on his own."

Nevia crossed her arms. "So, just sit down and shut up?"

Daniel groaned, feeling the entrapment of that statement. "Do you have any idea how much that woman hates you?" He pointed to the door.

"So what?" She shrugged. "I hate her too."

"Yes, but she's a fem-wolf, with lots of fem-wolf friends. Hunters don't hunt fem-wolves for a reason. The last thing we need is for you to piss off the entire council. We don't want to be the hunted."

"I'm sorry if my political views are getting in the way of your easy lifestyle."

"Fuck you!" Daniel turned away to get his anger under control. He could hear Nevia stomp toward the door. "Don't you dare leave now," he bristled, without looking at her. "You cast that stone and I'm not finished responding to it."

He heard her stop, and he finished his breathing so he didn't inadvertently hurt her. When he finally came to face her, her stoic face and rigid back were no less stubborn than they had ever been. "I have very few friends in this world, but I think I've made it abundantly clear in our short acquaintance that I want you to be listed among them. My friends get nothing less than my indisputable allegiance. I wouldn't think for a second about standing in the path of a bullet for those two men out there." Daniel jutted his finger out to indicate the two specific men he meant. When he found his finger connected to a shaky hand, he pulled it back in.

"My concern with your actions is based on their safety as well as yours. It has *nothing*..." Daniel paused to let the volume come under control. "...to do with my *easy* lifestyle. I'm just asking you not to start a war with the Council of the Moon. I don't think that's an unreasonable request."

Nevia relaxed slightly and nodded. "It's not an unreasonable request. You're right to ask it of me, but I would like to know where things stand between us if I can't meet that request."

Daniel felt the last bit of anger release from him. He wanted so much for this to be a little tiff that they would simply kiss and make up for later. Maybe it still could be if he could just get over it, but that wasn't likely to happen.

Daniel rubbed his forehead before approaching her. He leaned down and kissed her. It wasn't a sweet, gentle goodbye kiss like it probably should have been. It was a sloppy, wet kiss that tormented both of them. When he pulled away, he let his hand trail from her chin to her chest before falling away.

"I don't know. Do what you got to do. Just don't expect me to be okay with you veering us into the path of an angry werewolf pack." Daniel didn't wait for her response, nor did she stop him to offer one, but the crossroads had been established and he was taking his way. He really hoped she followed, but that wasn't likely to happen. After all, her independence was her most attractive quality.

27

E THAN WATCHED DANIEL RETURN to the bleachers without Nevia. He took his original seat between him and Heaton and stared off into nothingness. The conversation had obviously not gone well. Heaton was not too shy to ask about it, though. "Well?"

"If this goes south, you may wish you had put in for a transfer," Daniel said. Ethan glanced at Heaton, but he had no response to that. "She's going to do whatever she wants to."

"Then she can take the heat for it," Heaton murmured. "I'm not about to fight off a pack of fem-wolves just because she has a political statement to make."

Ethan leaned back to observe the trial. He didn't want to admit to Daniel and Heaton that he agreed with Nevia. He wasn't sure why she was so devoted to the cause, but even after spending a short amount of time with Callin, he knew he was a good man. He was a better father than most men, and indefensibly devoted to Leona. If he could do anything to help Callin, he would.

Nevia arrived back some time after the full roll of the trial had ensued. The look she gave Daniel suggested she felt guilty about something, but at the same time had no intention of not doing what she was feeling guilty for.

She sat for several minutes, looking at the seat beside her like she was keeping Daniel in her peripheral. Ethan wasn't sure what was going through her mind, but he was sure that he had seen it before. It was the same look Cori had given him before General Clark's men dragged her away. Nevia was begging for forgiveness, but to his knowledge, she hadn't done what she needed forgiveness for.

Ethan slid down the bleachers and took position behind her. She glanced at him, but continued to look forward. He leaned in so he could speak quietly. "Jordan," he said, despite already having her full attention by being inches from her ear. "I completely support Callin in his efforts. I don't know how to make that happen, but if I can do anything, I will. I know you feel the same way."

Nevia turned back slightly just to let him know he was right.

"However," Ethan let the word stand like it was its own sentence. "I get the feeling you are exploring rather extreme measures to achieve that support." Her ear dipped back enough to hint at the impact his words were having. "So, I'm just going to remind you that you are still an employee of this facility. You can decide where that puts you on the totem pole in relation to me, but the only thing you need to know for certain is that I am responsible for keeping the peace here. So, in case I'm right about the thoughts wandering through your mind right now, let me make something abundantly clear. If you so much as pull that firearm without an immediate threat, warranting it, you will either end up in a jail cell or in the infirmary. Do I make myself understood?" She lowered her head and exhaled.

"Yes, sir." He expected to hear a note of irritation in her voice, but it sounded more like relief.

Ethan crawled back up to his perch, where two querying faces eagerly waited to be filled in. He ignored both of them and put his attention back on the trial.

28

THE TRIAL WENT ON without the grandstanding that Ethan had heard about the day before. In the end, the leader of the council denied Callin's request to have his child. As the room of observers and most of the council members dispersed, Nevia leaped up the steps to him.

"Leona," she said with wide eyes. "She is considering letting Callin have the child in secret." She whispered, trying to be quiet despite her enthusiasm for her discovery.

Daniel and Heaton leaned over to her. Neither one actually said it, but their faces were begging her to let it go. He couldn't blame them. This was a dangerous road.

"What are you suggesting we do to encourage that?" he asked, ignoring the subtle head shakes his friends were offering.

"I don't want to encourage that. She needs to openly deny the council's right to decide who her children can be with. Otherwise, nothing will change."

"Nevia, let it go," Daniel pleaded.

"I can't, not when I can make a lasting change with a few well-placed observations. She is right on the precipice." Nevia's eyes pleaded back at him just as hard. "Callin is right. She will be the determining factor. She needs to take her sister's place. The council needs to have a coup."

"Ethan, this isn't our world," Heaton advised. "Trespassing on their traditions and beliefs is like walking into a holy war without a god. You can't convince anyone of anything when they think you're a heathen."

"Duly noted," Ethan said to Heaton before returning his attention to Nevia. "Come with me. Follow my lead and keep your comments obscure and naïve."

Ethan saw his opportunity and jumped on it. Frederique had just joined Leona and picked up Lynnius. Since she hadn't touched the baby before this, he assumed it was only to rub it in Callin's face rather than the enjoyment of it. The look on her face when she found out that he was a drooling baby confirmed that suspicion.

"May I?" he asked as he approached during the inevitable hand back. Both women paused in mid-pass and exchanged looks. "My wife and I are considering the leap ourselves," he added to soften his purpose.

"Of course." Frederique smiled and handed him the baby, who was already experimenting with sounds. "Human men are often excellent caretakers. I encourage it." She probably meant it as a slight against male werewolves, but since she didn't specifically exclude them, he just thanked her for the compliment.

"Hello, Lynnius, good to see you again." He cooed for a moment at the child. Lynnius was in an especially talkative mood and spluttered something along the lines of "pppblblbllestt" at him. Speckles of saliva danced the distance between Lynnius's lips and his shirt, but he just laughed. Unlike his frigid Auntie Frederique, Ethan was not afraid of a little drool. Drinking dragon sperm every day tends to harden one's stomach.

"Is it Lady Van Dorn?" he asked Frederique. She nodded. "I'm Ethan Pierce." He freed a hand up to shake hers. "I'm head of the guards and successor to the warden. I apologize for not being able to attend yesterday. We've had a rather spirited few days."

"I understand. It may have been for the best. At any rate, your friend seemed to do just fine." Frederique glanced back at Daniel, who had moved to the middle of the room with Heaton. They both looked alert and ready to save the day if necessary. He smiled at both of them. They were good friends.

"Yes." Ethan turned back to the conversation at hand. "I'm glad that things went better today. Although, I must say, I am a little disappointed with the results."

Frederique smiled, not willing to offer any comment that might indulge his opinions.

"Callin is a good man. Even as a potential father, I can't imagine not being with my children."

"Of course not, but you are not a risk to your child," Frederique stated with firm intention.

"Right, but if Callin enters into our program, we could make certain that he is away from his offspring during his phase."

"That argument has already been made and rejected. It really doesn't matter, anyway. He is in jail."

"Oh, not for long," Ethan said. "He isn't a criminal."

"He was forming a pack," Frederique snarled.

"Actually," Nevia jumped in. She looked at Ethan for a reproof, but he turned and offered her an inquisitive look that begged for her to tell him more. "The law strictly forbids packs to form under alpha males. As I observed yesterday, Callin specifically offered *Leona* the leadership of the pack."

"That's an interesting point, Jordan. I'll have to bring that to Danato's attention."

"The restriction on packs is a blanket law." Frederique didn't bother giving Nevia any eye contact. She may as well have been wearing a scarlet letter on her chest.

"Actually," Nevia offered again, and Ethan hid his smile, "I've read the laws numerous times, and the only definition I've found describing a pack suggests that four or more adult males conspiring to hunt live game, human or otherwise, is illegal."

"Interesting," Ethan said without any acting needed. "As I recall, and I think Leona can attest to it." Leona shriveled under his attention to her; it was an unusual sight to see, but if she was indeed on the precipice of being a decent person, he wasn't about to cut her any slack. "The only live game in Callin's home was the mold living on the leftover pizza."

Frederique glanced at Leona, but her sister's coy face said it all. She wouldn't say anything that would anger her. "This is all a moot point, Mr. Pierce."

"Ethan, please. I'm sure it is, but perhaps you would indulge me. I'm only beginning to understand your rules. What exactly has to change for Callin to be legally free to see his child?"

"The law," Frederique said with a "no duh" brow lift.

"No." Nevia's voice carried a blow that finally broke Frederique's resolve to appear civil and disinterested in her.

"You need to keep your half-breed mouth shut," she snapped with intensity more than volume.

"I believe you call my kind *mixed*," she said. Ethan felt like he had missed a step in the conversation, but resisted the urge to beg for answers. "To answer your question, Ethan, the law doesn't have to change, because the laws are based on historical doctrine that never changes. It only takes the leader of the Council of Moon to designate the change. What needs to change is the head council member."

"Tread lightly, small one," Frederique warned. Ethan got the distinct impression that if Frederique's eyes were capable of glowing, they would have.

Nevia looked at Leona. "The council may overthrow their leader if they can agree on who should take her place. The role is traditionally passed to the next of kin."

"Your efforts are fruitless," Frederique said, clutching her sister's shoulder. "My sister would never betray me." Leona winced slightly at the increasing grip on her shoulder. Frederique's statement was looking more and more like a threat.

Nevia looked them both over carefully. "That was before she became a mother, before she could see the future beyond her own lifespan." Leona watched Nevia with the same curiosity that everyone did when they were trying to decide if she was psychic or just really intuitive. "That was before she fell in love." Leona's face blanched, and she looked away, trying to hide that truth.

Frederique narrowed her eyes, but made no attempts to attack. "Do you know what a fem-wolf does to humans who cross her?" Nevia didn't waver. "I'll give you a hint; it's humane compared to what I do to mixed breeds."

"Lady Van Dorn," Ethan said. "I think we should wrap this up before anyone says or does anything they regret."

"I think the regret part has come and gone, she just doesn't recognize it yet. Come on, Leona." Frederique's shoes clacked away, but when Leona didn't follow immediately, she looked back.

"I'm coming," Leona said. "I just need to gather my children." Frederique looked at Lynnius still in Ethan's arms, as if she had forgotten he was there. She didn't bother to offer any help before storming away.

"Please tell me you see it now," Callin called over from his cell. Leona looked over to him. "We can't go on like this. Broken families have better social structure than us."

Ethan looked between them. When it was clear that Leona's cowardice was still winning, he moved to Callin's cell and unlocked it. Callin's bafflement lasted only a moment before he left the confinement. He paused to look at Lynnius and offered Ethan a less-than-gentle pat on the back.

He greeted Leona with a heated kiss that steered Nevia away from them. Daniel and Heaton followed her lead, disappearing around the corner, while Ethan played nanny to their make-out session—a contribution he hadn't really intended to make, but Lynnius's high-pitched squeal and garbled, enthusiastic blubbers, told him *he* had no objections to the arrangement.

29

As far as Daniel was concerned, there weren't enough eye daggers to be thrown. Even with Heaton's reinforcement, the elevator seemed to be lacking the hostility he wanted to express to Nevia. She stood at the back of the elevator with her arms crossed, looking anywhere but at them. Heaton and he exchanged glances, but neither of them wanted to start the tirade. Heaton no doubt felt it should be him. He really needed to check with Ethan to see if it was a standard protocol in these situations for the boyfriend to engage in disciplinary actions.

"You can both stop the glaring," Nevia snarled. "I hardly need the visual confirmation. I already smell your annoyance."

"This is not simply annoyance," Heaton said, moving toward her. Though Daniel knew he wouldn't hurt her, he flinched at the movement. "You have made yourself an enemy of the Council of the fucking Moon. Do you know how much danger you have put yourself in? And by association, us?"

"Yes, but do you not see the bigger picture here?"

"No, all I see is *your* picture—*your* goal, *your* purpose." Heaton looked at Daniel. There was a question in his eyes, but he had no idea what it was. "You've used this opportunity to settle a dispute of your own creation. We will have no part in the ramifications of it. Until an official replacement can be found, I will recommend to Sophie that you take a paid leave of absence. You are no longer welcome on this team."

Daniel wasn't sure what to offer to the situation. He wanted to defuse it, but at the same time he didn't want to suggest to Nevia that he wasn't mad about her actions. Before he could make a decision, the elevator doors opened and Heaton stepped out.

Nevia quickly followed. The spiraling situation left Daniel fumbling through his mind for words, let alone to find the enthusiasm to leap after the two of them. Nevia stood her ground in the main foyer, where Heaton was slipping on his coat. Daniel kept his distance from both of them.

"Don't do this," Nevia said.

"You've left me no choice!" Heaton yelled. "We can't function as a team if we are spending as much time fending off fem-wolves as looking for our targets."

"That's not why you're doing this."

"What are you talking about?" Heaton's face scrunched up in further aggravation.

"Why are you forcing him to choose between us?" Nevia said.

Daniel wasn't sure what Nevia had sensed from Heaton, but the statement stopped him in his tracks.

"You think he'll choose to stay partnered with you and endure the repeated werewolf attacks that you've brought on?" Heaton scoffed. "I doubt it."

"No, I think you plan to subtly convince him that if he doesn't stay with me that I'll wind up getting myself killed." Heaton's jaw went slack. There was no need for lie detectors when Nevia was around. "You would manipulate his loyalties until he decided it was for the best to stay with me while you go onto a new team. Which is what you wanted all along, because you are too much of a coward to be honest with your own friend."

"What is she talking about?" Daniel asked, approaching Heaton.

"This has nothing to do with me," Heaton assured her. "This is about you picking fights with the wrong people and endangering us."

"Yes, but your reaction seems too calculated to be honestly come to. At this point, you would use any situation to force a wedge into this team. Anything to give you the freedom to abandon it without recrimination."

"You lied," Daniel said. Heaton looked at him even though he was still trying to maintain the argument with Nevia. "You are still trying to get transferred."

"Daniel... It's complicated," Heaton said as guilt washed over his face.

"I thought we were friends. Feck, I thought we were brothers."

"I'm not trying to hurt you. I just don't want to change what we have."

"You've been..." Daniel looked down. He wasn't sure how to describe the relationship he had with Heaton. He was a friend and family, but also his balance. Belus may have gotten him on track to becoming a better person, but Heaton was the one who kept him steady and forced him back on track when he got out of line.

Heaton was still struggling to offer an explanation, but Daniel didn't hear any of it. All he heard were excuses for his abandonment and rejection. It was just enough to tip the scales. Not on his temper, but on hurt. He could have walked away from Nevia forever at that moment and still not felt the anguish of his friend wanting to leave him.

It was too much.

Heaton couldn't have predicted that Daniel would punch him over the slight. Despite his so-called gift, Daniel had never been a fighter. He was far more likely to take a punch and pretend to be passed out than actually engage in the barbaric display. He told himself that he didn't have the skill to fight, but given that Heaton's body flew back several feet from the impact, he decided there probably wasn't as much skill required as he thought.

The expression on Heaton's face behind his blood-probing hand said that he was just as insulted by the attack as Daniel was by his breach of friendship. He set his jaw and lunged back at Daniel. As much as Heaton probably wanted to settle the matter diplomatically, he couldn't let the assault go unanswered for. His pride was far greater than Daniel's and with his masculinity in question, he wouldn't be satisfied until he had proved himself superior to—or at the very least, equal to—the aggressor.

Daniel flew back from Heaton's tackle. Nevia jumped out of their way, barely avoiding getting wrapped up in the brawl. Heaton pushed Daniel into the railing of the short stairs preceding the office hallway. Daniel hoped Danato wasn't around. He would likely blame him for the violence, no matter how bad Heaton bruised his face.

Heaton's first official punches landed in quick succession in his stomach. He did his best to tighten his muscles, but the first blow had already tenderized them. Daniel shoved him away with more strength than Heaton was prepared for. He stumbled to the floor.

Daniel took the opportunity to get the upper hand, but Heaton kicked him with the heel of his shoe before he could. Heaton adeptly flipped himself from the floor into a standing crouch. He punched Daniel in the face. It didn't feel good, but Daniel got the impression that Heaton was holding back. The gesture did nothing to soften Daniel's resolve, though. He punched him back, nicking his jaw.

They both paused for a moment. Questioning the next step. They could either stop the battle there and discuss this as gentlemen, or they could throw away everything and once and for all decide who the better man was. Naturally, they decided to brawl out their differences.

Nevia had been yelling in the background the whole time. Daniel hadn't been listening since he was otherwise occupied, but somewhere in the middle of their wrestling match, he had managed to get the upper hand and wasn't quite sure what to do with it.

"Just tell him the truth, Heaton!" she yelled.

Heaton's legs wrapped around Daniel's and he was a moment away from regaining a dominant position, but he paused a moment after that statement. Daniel panted overtop his friend, squishing his cheeks into his eyes with his left hand, while his right hand struggled to keep Heaton from ripping out his hair. Thankfully, neither of them skirted the line of actually trying to choke the other.

In that hesitated moment, Daniel saw how ridiculous they both looked wrapped up in each other like a pretzel. He remembered another reason he didn't like fighting. No matter how tough the guys were, they always ended up looking like two little kids fighting over a piece of candy. The word immature didn't translate when the pain of fist blows was fresh, but all coiled up on the floor with the high of aerobic exertion offering clarity, he felt juvenile.

He released Heaton's face and rolled off him. He sat on the floor and cussed a few times just to give himself a moment to think before he spoke again. Heaton stood up and looked at him. If there was an apology to be said, it wouldn't be said yet, but for the moment, a truce had been reached.

"I'm sorry," Nevia offered the apology. They both looked at her, baffled. Not only was she placing the apology too early by any male standards, she was also offering it without cause. "This is all my fault," she said.

"How's that?" Daniel asked. He noticed his bulbous lip. It tasted like blood. He wondered if it was possible to use his power on himself.

"You two wouldn't be in this situation if it weren't for me. I've made you question your friendship."

"He made me question it, not you." Daniel nodded to Heaton, offering him a glare that he mirrored back to him.

"I'm the reason he's leaving, Daniel, not you."

Daniel furrowed his brow and looked between them. "What the feck is going on between you two? What did I miss?" He shrugged. "If I'm getting in the way of something, you should have told me." Neither of them offered confirmation or denial. "Fine," he stood up and dusted himself off, as if the glaring white floors actually had dirt. "Just keep your little secrets. Neither of you needs to transfer. I'll check with Danato about finding a new parole officer." He glared at Heaton as he walked over to the steps leading to Danato's office.

"Tell him!" Nevia's voice filled the room. He was impressed she could muster so much volume from her tiny body. He looked back at Heaton. He looked guilty again, and a little scared. "This has gone too far. He thinks we are conspiring against him. The damage made by telling your secret is small in comparison to the damage it is doing by keeping it." Nevia waited for Heaton to say something, but when he made no attempts to stop her approach to Daniel, she blurted out the long-held secret.

"Heaton's gay." She hissed it like it was still a secret they should keep the walls from hearing.

"What?"

Daniel was thinking it, but it was actually Ethan that said it as he came off the elevator.

30

To say he had missed something was an understatement. Ethan could see the bloody noses and freshly bluing bruises on his friends. He had only just overheard the mention of the secret to be revealed. Upon its revelation, he was shocked enough to question it.

"What?"

Everyone looked over at him, noting his arrival. Heaton was not happy to see him, and cussed under his breath as he turned away from all of them.

Daniel laughed, drawing Nevia's attention back to him. "Heaton's not gay. I've known the guy for five years. I would know if he were gay."

Ethan looked at Heaton for confirmation, but he offered nothing more than disappointment. Somehow, the conversation they had the other day was making sense. Heaton was worried about telling his secret because it would change how they saw him. Given that Daniel was his closest friend, it would follow that he would be most affected by the revelation.

Nevia shrugged. "I'm sorry, Heaton. I can't let you destroy your friendship over something as trivial as your sexual preference."

Heaton turned to her. "But it's okay to irreparably transform it into a fraction of its former self!"

"You're not gay," Daniel insisted, as if Heaton were merely mistaken. "You go home with women all the time."

"I leave the bar with women all the time. I generally walk them home, because unlike the men in the bar trying to get into their pants, I am genuinely a gentleman."

"No, you're not! You..." Daniel blinked several times, then scoffed with no particular purpose other than to express his disillusionment.

Heaton looked at Ethan. "What do you have to say?"

Ethan felt blindsided by the question, like he had been called on to give an oral report. "Umm, congratulations?"

Heaton glared at him. "I'm not coming out, you twat. I've been out since I was sixteen."

"Then why didn't you tell me?" he asked, feeling the betrayal of Heaton's omission.

"I didn't tell you because I hadn't told him." He nodded to Daniel.

"Why didn't you tell him?" Ethan asked.

Daniel moved closer to him and crossed his arms to wait for that same answer.

"First, it was inappropriate information to share. Then it was unnecessary. Then it was just none of his business." Heaton glared at Daniel, but it faded quickly. "Then..." He looked away.

"Oh, good Lord," Daniel cringed. "Are you in love with me?"

Nevia chuckled, and Heaton crinkled his nose at him. "Dude!"

"What? Isn't that a logical chain of events?" Daniel motioned to himself as if he were clearly irresistible.

"Yeah, if I didn't think you were a complete ass, which I do. So no, I'm not in love with you. I was going to say that our partnership became invaluable, and I thought that my revealing my homosexuality to someone who was so grandly heterosexual might make you uncomfortable. I kept it out of common knowledge to keep our work life easy, and then I just didn't want to ruin our friendship."

Daniel thought about that for a moment. His anger was fading, but he still looked hurt. "So, you're saying, in the entire five years of our employment together... You never once thought about shagging me."

Heaton groaned and Ethan stifled his laughter along with Nevia. "I—you—no!" Heaton stuttered, flummoxed by Daniel's change of direction.

"Why not?"

"Dude, I have taste. You aren't my type, and frankly, your enthusiasm for the opposite sex kind of puts off even the remotest thought of—what difference does it make? You aren't gay!"

"If *I* was gay, I would totally want *you*. Wouldn't *you*, Ethan?" Daniel threw the question at him like he was supposed to be offering support to their newly crippled gay friend.

He waved his hands in surrender. "Don't put me in the middle of this."

"Daniel, don't you have anything serious to say about this?" Heaton asked, returning to his calm demeanor. Ethan could sense the levity Daniel was using to make the situation bearable fade away.

"About what?" Daniel asked. "About you trying to abandon your best friend just so you can go be gay in peace without the burden of my presumed judgment looming over you? I do have something to say about that, but since we've already beaten the snot out of each other, let's just draw an arrow from this conversation back to five minutes ago, when I first punched you in the face." Daniel walked away, but turned back, unsatisfied with his departing words.

"Did you really think ditching me was better? What did you think I was going to do if you told me the truth? Nag you about your hair and call you a poof? Oh, wait, I do that already. It actually takes the fun out of it now. I would lay down my life for you two." Daniel looked at Ethan to include him. "Did you think I would recant that level of loyalty just because you want to have a boyfriend instead of a girlfriend?"

"I never questioned your loyalty, Daniel," Heaton said, closing the distance between them. "I just didn't want..." He motioned to the space between them. "...this to change. I didn't want to lose what made this work."

"Well, of course it's going to change." Daniel furrowed his brow in disapproval. "I'm going to be calling you a poof a lot more and I'm going to make fun of your hair and clothes more." Even though Daniel was trying to bring back the humor to the situation, his face didn't show it yet.

Heaton chuckled. "I'm not quite sure why I would have expected any less."

Daniel shook his head, approaching Heaton. "Because you're an eejit." He gave Heaton a bear hug that prompted a less enthusiastic back pat from Heaton. When he finally released him, Daniel narrowed his eyes at him suspiciously. "Not once?" he asked.

"Dude," Heaton grumbled.

Ethan looked at Nevia, who had a pleased smile on her face. "I take it you knew about this already?"

"I hate secrets," she said, losing her smile.

He was about to ask why she had such a strong aversion to secrets when the lights flickered and went out.

31

DANATO CUSSED IN THE pitch black. He grabbed the walkie-talkie and called for his maintenance department, who doubled as dock personnel. After a minute, the device squawked and someone came on the line.

"Boss, we're working on it." The voice sounded breathy, like the man had been running.

"I hope to hell so. It's pitch black in here. Why isn't the back-up generator turning on?"

"There's been an overload or something. We're still determining why the backup hasn't turned on. I'll let you know more in a few minutes when I reach the sub-basement and get a look at the grid." The radio clicked off.

Danato reached for the phone and blindly dialed Belus's extension. He picked up after the first ring, as if he had been waiting by the phone. Since he was waiting for news about Cori's situation, he probably was.

"Yeah," he said gruffly.

"Belus, the power is out."

"What? How the hell..." He trailed off, no doubt realizing that if Danato knew the why of the situation, he would already be fixing it. "What about the backup?"

"It hasn't come on yet. I take it your power is fine."

"Yeah."

"Hopefully that means my house is still powered."

"That won't be enough energy to satisfy her for long." Concern started to bleed into Belus's voice. He knew as well as Danato that a power outage was not something the prison could afford. At least not for long.

"I know. They're working on it."

"If she isn't satisfied—"

"I know, Belus! Look, just get over to the house and check things out. Then get in here. I've got fem-wolves and military maniacs running around my prison and no light to keep an eye on them."

"On my way." Belus hung up before Danato could thank him.

32

"D ON'T TELL ME YOU didn't pay your light bill," Daniel said when the lights shut down. The unexpected power outage left everyone frozen in place. The lack of windows left the area completely dark, but after a few seconds, Daniel's eyes adjusted and he could see as if he were wearing night vision goggles. The colors didn't come through, but he could at least make out the majority of the shapes.

"This has never happened before." Ethan scrambled for his radio and called his men for an explanation.

Heaton found a wall to lean against. Even in the dark, with no one watching, he looked casual and cool. Nevia, on the other hand, looked positively panicked. She was flailing her hands as if she expected someone to jump out at her in the dark.

"What the hell is the point of being a quarter werewolf if you can't even see in the dark or run worth a damn?"

"What?" Ethan asked, since he had missed out on that part of Nevia's background.

"I can smell," she retorted. "What more do you want? I suppose you can see just fine?"

Daniel didn't bother responding. He snuck in behind her, clear of her probing hands, and wrapped his arms around her. She yelped and elbowed him, but when he didn't let go, she relaxed against him. He put the trial to the back of his mind for the moment and nuzzled into her neck.

She smelled good—like baby powder. Yet another soft contradiction to her hard personality. She kept him guessing. He hated that, but only because he loved it.

"No making out, you two," Heaton stated sleepily from his wall.

"What?" Ethan's voice pitched at yet another nugget of missed information. "Crap, you guys. You gotta keep me in the loop."

The radio clicked and Duke came on the line, cheerful as always. "Wooo-weeee! It's darker than a black Angus tookus in here."

"Tell me about it," Ethan responded. "Why is it dark?"

"Don't know yet," Duke said. "Maintenance is checking the lines. Better get your flashlight out for now."

Ethan winced and started patting his canvas pants. He pulled a small LED flashlight from his pocket and turned it on. The light shined on each of them as Ethan checked their positions. Daniel released Nevia before Ethan caught them in the embrace. He had no intention of hiding the relationship, but he sensed that PDA was not Nevia's style.

"Any orders, Boss?" Duke asked.

"I need to check in with Danato. In the meantime, get down to two and find out how long the power can be off on the habitat environments before the animals are in danger."

"Will do." Duke clicked off and Ethan headed toward Danato's office. Heaton followed behind him, staying with the light. Daniel headed up with them, but stopped to check on Nevia. Even with Ethan's flashlight guiding their direction, she was still agitated.

He took a chance and slipped his hand into hers to tow her along. To his surprise, she gripped his hand tightly, trusting him to be her eyes.

33

CORI WASN'T SURE WHEN the dinner party had started or why she was so late, but she was vaguely aware that her blue jean attire was not satisfactory to the pretentious guests she passed by. She weaved through the clusters of elitists who made expensive suits and ornate hats look better than the mannequins that displayed them.

The cocktail hour was in full swing and she was certain she needed to find something. She couldn't remember what it was, but it seemed important enough to hurry for. She grabbed a champagne flute from a passing waiter to better blend in with the crowd. She sipped the sour pink liquid, but it seemed resistant to quenching her thirst, despite being a liquid.

She was about to give up hope of finding what it was she didn't know she was looking for when she saw a familiar face leaning against the mantle of a fireplace on the far side of the room. His tall, slender body filled his suit better than she would have expected. He looked well-fed and atypically sun-touched. His hands gripped a glass of brown liquor as if it were an extension of his hand. His hair should have been down, but for once it was back, offering him the slick regal look that would make many mistake him for a vampire.

She meandered over to the lounge area where three men were drinking in his words, like students of their favorite professor. Cleos said something, and they all laughed. He smiled at his own joke, but as he noticed her approach, it faded. She hated that so much.

Despite his lack of pleasure in seeing her, she smiled cordially at him. His eyes looked her over in that almost sexual way and she couldn't help but be relieved by the familiar greeting.

"Gentlemen, would you excuse us?" Cleos said. She expected him to usher her away to speak in private, but it was the men who left. She stepped forward, taking a seat on the cold leather couch that Cleos proffered. "What are you doing here?" he asked, as if she had just let herself into his home without knocking.

Cori looked around and then at her hand. She was still holding the displeasing pink drink. "Drinking. It's a party, isn't it?" she said, offering the obvious when another answer didn't readily come to mind.

"Yes." His conformation soothed her confusion. "But why are you here? You shouldn't be here."

"I didn't have time to dress," she said, looking down at her clothes. She was never one to dress up, but she really wished she would have made the effort to look nice. She didn't want to embarrass Cleos in front of his guests.

"No, I imagine not," he said sympathetically before sitting on the coffee table in front of her. His choice of seat seemed to offend the stiff upper-class citizens, who wouldn't deign to sit on a toilet unless it had been cleaned by an underpaid minority. "Darling, give me your hand."

"Yes, Jim dear," Cori said, following it with a gleaming smile, but he didn't seem to get the joke. She placed her hand in his, and his brow lifted high. He shook his head.

"Oh Cori, you are the very definition of Murphy's Law." He kissed her hand. "You are a beautiful mind, and I would love nothing more than to drink you in and add you to my collection, but..." He took in a deep breath and looked around the room at his guests. "No," he said resolutely before turning back to her. "It's not good that you're here. You shouldn't be here," he said sternly.

"Where is here?" Cori looked around the room.

"My mind."

"You've entered my mind?"

"No, you have entered mine," he scolded.

She looked around the room, trying to figure out why there was a dinner party going on in his mind. "How is that possible?"

"You shouldn't have opened your eyes."

Cori looked down at her rings. She *was* the very definition of Murphy's Law. "I'm in trouble, aren't I?"

"I imagine, since you are probably unconscious. Do you remember anything before you were here?"

"No." Cori sighed. "I was in my cell. Then I was here. Why is there a dinner party in your mind?"

Cleos smiled and drew his finger down her cheek. She knew she probably sounded naïve, but it was her first time being inside of someone's mind. She was allowed a few dumb questions.

"It's not so much a dinner party as my trophy case."

"Trophies?" She looked around at the people. "Are these all your victims?"

"Not the way you think." Cleos stood and joined her on the couch. She leaned back, tucking her leg beneath her so she could face him. "They are my revenge collection."

"Revenge? That doesn't sound good."

"You can raise your expectations of me as high as you want, but I am still a criminal. Some of my crimes are more heinous than others, but I've never regretted any of them."

"What are they?" Cori asked, looking around the room again.

"They are egos, character flaws, and obsessions." He didn't take his eyes off her as he spoke. He watched her react to everything he said. "Many people have underestimated me. My photophobic condition leaves me with a very specific social life. Would you believe that I am filthy rich?"

Cori smirked at him. "Yes."

"Yes?" He perked an eyebrow. "What's my tell?"

"You're snooty." She bit her lip, hoping the blunt interpretation wouldn't insult him.

"Snooty? My apologies, I was going for refined."

"Refined yes, but snooty too." She giggled, and he finally smiled back at her.

"As I was saying, I'm filthy rich. My wealth is all legal on paper, but the means that I have come about my fortune has more to do with my powers of persuasion than my skill at business."

"You manipulated these people into making business deals."

Cleos pulled his arm over the back of the sofa and repositioned to face her straight-on. "In business, it's about knowing your opponent and capitalizing on their weaknesses. I don't need to find anyone's weaknesses; I can create them.

"With a little time and effort, I can remove entire personality profiles. I can rip away part of a man's character, leaving him without the drive to succeed, or even the will to live." Cori frowned. "I've never done that. I'm just telling you what I'm capable of." Cleos winked, but she didn't find the subject matter playful enough to warrant it. "These people are character aspects. They are repetitive, cyclical shells of the people they used to belong to, and they are my trophies."

Cori looked around the room again, seeing the judgmental, self-involved crowd in a different light.

"I can eliminate their need to please others. I can take away the source of addictions and obsessions. I can even take away a man's self-assurance, making him meek as a mouse, and easily intimidated."

"So, these aren't the whole person's mind, just the part of their personality that might prevent you from getting money from them."

"Now you're getting it."

"You're not really one of the good guys, are you?" she murmured.

"Never was, Cori. You're going to have to accept that at some point."

Cori shook her head, even though she knew he was right. She had to stop pretending that Cleos had a good heart. He may not be the evil incarnate that Ethan and Danato thought he was, but he was still a selfish, manipulative crook.

"So, how do I get out of here?" she asked, happily changing the subject.

"You will wake up."

"Why am I unconscious? I don't remember anything."

"I imagine that whoever knocked you out probably did a number on your short-term memory."

Cori furrowed her brow as she started to understand the nature of her situation. "*Someone* knocked me out. Oh, no. Clark. He's taking me from the prison. I have to wake up." Cori still couldn't remember what had happened to her, but she remembered the urgency she felt when she first arrived at the party. "I have to get out of here. I have to wake up." Cori stood up as if she might simply search for an exit to leave Cleos's mind.

Cleos stood and blocked her immediate flight. "When you wake, you may not remember this, or at least you'll think it was a dream. It's important that you come and tell me about this, because the real me won't know about this. Not until you tell him."

"Oh, crap, don't tell me: if I don't get out of your head, I'll be lobotomized."

"Actually, I have no idea what will happen, but let's face it, with your predilection to lethal levels of bad luck, I would advise keeping your unconscious mind in your own head."

Cori nodded in agreement as she felt the intensity in her need to flee finally pay off. Cleos faded away, as did his trophy room. Only the faint smell of leather, the hardwood floor, and the dull ache in her head told her she had arrived back in the real world.

34

"REPORT," DANATO BARKED EVEN before Ethan had made it through the door. Heaton and Daniel followed right after him, but Nevia waited in the hallway. She seemed reluctant to give up her gun, and was effectively standing guard at the door. It would have been more comforting if she wasn't blindly searching for the doorjamb as a point of reference.

"I knew you were on a budget, Danato, but—" Daniel started to joke. Ethan didn't bother letting him get them too far off the subject when this was clearly an abnormal situation.

"I sent Duke to medical to see if the animals are going to be in danger without power. Otherwise, I came straight here." Ethan sat down, placing the flashlight across Danato's desk so they had marginal light for their conversation.

"Good thinking. Belus is checking on... something, but he'll be over soon. I should have word from maintenance on the cause of all this soon." Even as Danato said it, the walkie-talkie crackled and a man on the other end cleared his throat.

"Ahh, Danato?"

"Report."

"Yeah, um, this is going to take us a little while to fix."

"Fix. What's wrong?"

"The main circuit breaker is fucked. I need to rewire the whole damn thing."

"Do it fast. What about the backup generators? Can't we get them started?"

"They've been compromised as well."

"Compromised how?" Danato asked.

"The wires have been melted down like solder, like they got... struck by lightning."

Danato lowered the radio to the desk, his eyes glazed in thought.

"Efrat?" Ethan wasn't willing to wait for Danato to verbalize his thoughts. "But why?"

"I don't know. I told him we would give them asylum."

"And they're likely to take you at your word?" Ethan asked. Danato grimaced. He clearly thought his word shouldn't be questioned. "They aren't really stable. Maybe they're taking an opportunity to get revenge on Clark and his men. You can't renege on your promise if Clark is already out of the picture."

Danato paused, thinking about that. "That's risky considering Clark is primed to shoot on sight, but you're right. They're unstable. They're already considering some hefty extremes to get their freedom." Danato picked up a pencil and tapped it relentlessly on his desk. Ethan waited for him to bark orders, but he didn't. "Something's missing," he mumbled. "It just doesn't make sense. They have what they want."

"Unless…" Ethan started, but the eagerness in Danato's face gave him pause. Danato usually didn't leave the reins to a crisis lying around. "Do you think Clark would go to this extreme? An elemental weapon would be just the thing to take out our wiring."

Danato nodded absentmindedly. "There's only one threat he's been waving in our faces."

Ethan jumped up before Danato gave the order. He was halfway down the hall, with Heaton on his tail, before he heard Danato barking into the radio for backup at Cori's location.

35

CORI LOOKED UP AT the high raftered ceiling of her home and momentarily hoped that it was all just a bad dream, but the duct tape holding her hands together over her head told her otherwise. The hair raised on her arm told her who, but it didn't tell her why.

That was the only question on her mind, and the only one she could verbalize. "Why?"

She lifted her head off the cold wood floor and saw Efrat side-saddled on the back of the couch. He managed to look comfortable despite the awkward position. He was holding his arms out, so he didn't shock himself. He looked like a surgeon, constantly trying to stay sterile.

She looked around the dimly lit room, but they were alone. She was once again surprised the house didn't prevent his entrance like it did for Belus, but she imagined carrying her unconscious body qualified him for entrance.

"Efrat, what's happened? Why am I here?" A brief hope crossed her mind. "Did you save me?" The scornful expression he offered her told her she was as naïve as he always accused her of being. "Efrat. What do you want?"

He clenched his jaw and took in a deep breath before speaking. "I used to be a good man, an honorable man. You saw that. I know you did. I was happy, healthy, and personable. Then this place." He clenched his fists and looked at them with revulsion. "I could have dealt with this. Over time, I know Dr. Frank would have figured something out. She would have fixed it."

Cori shifted, testing her restraints, but the tape was too thick to break. She couldn't direct her power with her hands together. Anything she released would just be reabsorbed. Efrat must have planned on that. Her best defense was also her greatest weakness.

"Clark keeps waiting for us to give in and become his weapons. All we want is a normal life, but he won't allow that. At least with Danato, we might have a chance."

"Danato is a good man, I promise. I wouldn't have placed your life in his hands if I didn't think he could protect you. Believe me, Efrat; I don't want to see anyone else die."

He stared blankly at her, like she was a television on mute.

"Dr. Frank had that same reverence for life. We used to call her Dr. Frankenstein." Efrat looked around the room like he hadn't had a chance to look at it yet. "She's gone now. There's only one option left for us to live a semi-normal life."

"What's that?" Cori asked.

"Remi and Garr are going to request amputations as soon as we are legally in Danato's custody."

Cori's mouth dropped open. Somewhere in the back of her mind, she knew Jill had considered that as a last resort, but it surprised her that anyone would volunteer for the procedure.

"Jill believed that with intensive training, you might be able to control the powers."

"Six years hasn't brought me any enlightenment. I don't plan on waiting another six to achieve it," Efrat snapped.

"Are you sure amputation is what you want?"

He pinned her with another glare she didn't imagine she deserved, but she wasn't sure he was capable of any other expression at the moment. "I'm not getting an amputation. I'll lose a hand in battle, but there is no way in hell I'm going to volunteer to lose it. Not if there's another option available." His glare faded, but the predatory gaze he offered in its place wasn't an improvement.

"What are you talking about?" She felt her voice slip into a whisper, like what he was about to say was a secret they should keep quiet.

"Your rings absorb my power quite well."

Cori nodded. She could feel tears well in her eyes as the fear started to set in more firmly. "But they don't come off. You tried yourself."

"Yes. I tried again while you were unconscious. They won't budge."

Cori blinked back her tears and shrugged. "Sorry. I would give them to you if I could."

"You still can."

She shook her head vigorously. "No, I can't. I don't know how."

Efrat reached for something on the sofa. As he drew up the large familiar cleaver that usually lay in a drawer because it was too big for the knife block, she let out a whimper.

36

ETHAN LATCHED ONTO GENERAL Clark's throat before either of them had a chance to insinuate guilt on the other. Heaton stood between him and one of Clark's men. Two soldiers were already laid out on the glossy concrete, one because of an ill-planned attack on Heaton that resulted in being flipped over Heaton's shoulder—he was still gasping for air. The other soldier was passed out when Ethan had arrived.

In the waning light of the high windows, Ethan could see Clark's sputtered profanities mist the air with saliva. He wasn't threatened by him, and he was tired of pretending that he was anyone of consequence to him. "Where is she?" He nodded to the open cell that Cori no longer occupied.

Clark choked out a few unintelligible words before Ethan lowered him enough to stand flat-footed. "I don't know," he rasped, trying to wrench from the steel-muscled noose.

"Bullshit." Ethan shoved him away and looked at the out-of-breath soldier behind him. "Where is my wife? So help me, somebody better talk, because I'm done with the paperwork part of this deal."

"We don't know! She was gone when we got here. The cell was open and Baker was passed out." The soldier gestured to the other guard on the floor.

"I presumed you had taken her," Clark said. "I was on my way to question you when you arrived. I was going to congratulate you on your sabotage ruse."

"It's not a ruse, it's Efrat," Ethan said without regard for the secrecy they maintained for hiding the elementals. If they were indeed behind this, he no longer cared about protecting them from Clark.

"Efrat?" Clark said.

"He fried the generators."

"He's here?" Clark said, more baffled than irritated by the statement.

"He's been here. We were going to offer them asylum, but if he's responsible for Cori going missing, then I'll hand him back to you on a silver platter."

"That's an interesting deal. Perhaps I should have been negotiating with *you* all along."

"Perhaps you should have," Ethan said with an even tone that made the conversation undercut Danato's authority even further.

"I'm not sure Danato would agree," Clark said with a slight smirk.

Ethan didn't respond. He couldn't outright disparage Danato to Clark. Somehow, that was going too far.

"Perhaps my men should assist with the search. After we find her, we can discuss my reward for helping you."

"Just one thing before I accept." Ethan waved over Daniel, who arrived late with Nevia in tow. As soon as they were bathed in the afternoon light from the windows, Nevia spotted the armed guard Heaton was protecting him from and she put him in the sight of her gun. The glare Clark offered her screamed his loathing for her impudence.

"What's the scoop, Ethan?" Daniel asked, noticing the open cell door.

"Cori's missing. Clark says he doesn't know anything about it. Jordan, why don't you get your lie detector over here?"

Nevia lowered her gun and approached Clark, but he pulled his pistol on her. She raised hers again and Ethan drew his as well. Overlooking itchy trigger fingers, everyone threw around a slew of demands.

Before any demands could be met or negotiated, the armed soldier covering Heaton flew halfway through the section, seemingly without cause. The demands stopped. Heaton and Ethan looked back at Daniel.

Daniel stepped up behind Nevia, towering over her, yet still behind her. He wore the same deathly dark expression on his face that he had during his last encounter with Clark. Ethan lowered his weapon in preparation to keep his friend from murdering Clark.

"Take your gun off her," Daniel said simply.

Nevia must have smelled the same danger from Daniel, because she also lowered her gun despite her head still being targeted by Clark.

"What kind of freak are you?" Clark glanced over Daniel's body as if it would punctuate the insult with an exclamation point, but the shake in his voice left it less than scathing.

"I'm the guy that just told you to lower your weapon."

Clark glanced at Ethan as if to check if Daniel was as dangerous as he seemed to be. Ethan gave a slight nod and made a point to show that he was also holstering his gun. Clark licked his lips nervously and put his away as well. Nevia was the last to holster, but she kept her arms crossed for easy access while she distantly sniffed the air around Clark.

"He's just as surprised by all this as we are," Nevia confirmed.

Clark's brow deepened in further confusion. "You're all freaks."

"Look at the employer," Heaton mumbled beside him.

Ethan ran his fingers over his hair and took in a few thought-clearing breaths. "Okay, Clark, here's the deal..." Ethan's radio squawked and Danato's grumbled voice came over. "Go ahead."

"I'm at the greenhouse. Garr and Remi are still here, but they said Efrat left an hour ago."

Clark's head tipped like he couldn't believe they were just a few hundred yards away from the prison.

"Did he tell them why?"

"No, just that he had to figure something out on his own. Apparently, he figured out how to hobble us. I can only assume he's trying to escape. How's Cori?"

Ethan sighed. Why was there never any good news about Cori? "Cori's missing."

There was a slight pause on the other end. "Did she..." was all that Danato could formulate. Given Cori's current resume, it wasn't outrageous for him to think Cori might help Efrat escape. Ethan hadn't considered that for a moment, but even as he did, he didn't want to believe it. Cori had too many marks in her *bad decision* column. He knew she wouldn't risk doing something stupid again so soon.

Then again.

"No," Ethan said with more confidence than he felt. "Cori's not *that* conniving. If anything, Efrat has talked her into or threatened her into helping him again. Or maybe he thinks he's helping her. No matter what the reason is, the first step is finding her."

Danato agreed and clicked off the radio.

"He thinks she's helping him escape again," Clark said, looking at his unconscious man.

"I don't think so, but Danato can't rule it out. We just can't think of any other reason for Efrat to take her."

"Perhaps they're running away together. They seemed quite close to me." Clark had started the statement with a hidden smile in his eyes, but as he finished, his eyes trailed to the floor in contemplation.

Ethan rolled his eyes. "Cori is not involved with Efrat." He couldn't even muster the anger to defend his wife. The suggestion was so preposterous. Cori loved him, and only him. She wouldn't betray him.

Efrat, on the other hand...

37

CORI KNEW FEAR. SHE understood it intimately. She could usually put on her tough face and muster through like she was brave, but deep down she understood that the bravado was just survival instincts at work. Watching Efrat come toward her with a cleaver in his hand was different. She wasn't feeling fear; she was feeling terror, and it paralyzed her.

Contrary to her experiences, Efrat wouldn't kill her or rape her. He was going to amputate her hands. She would survive it, but it was going to be unimaginable pain, and for no other reason than a set of gold rings with magical powers. Powers that would fail miserably against sharpened steel.

The strange part was, Efrat wasn't snarling maniacally at her. He was approaching slowly and speaking quietly, as if he could stave off her fear with placidity. He was explaining why he was going to cut off her hands rather than her fingers—something about a lesser degree of mutilation because it would only take one strike. She stopped listening when she realized he wasn't just threatening to do this to get her to give up the rings. He actually intended to do it.

That was perhaps the strangest realization ever: the epiphany that no matter how much she had done to protect him, he still didn't give a damn about her.

She let her head sink back against the wood floor, and she stared at the ceiling. She was sure she was supposed to be doing something: screaming, negotiating, or struggling, but she didn't have the energy for it.

She was tired of fighting Efrat. She was tired of trying to help him, too. She may not be able to stop him from cutting off her hands, but in doing so, he was signing his own death warrant, and she no longer cared if he lived or died.

38

"Is it Efrat?" Ethan asked before Nevia could reveal her finding in the cell.

Daniel leaned in behind him, just as eager to get the answer. Nevia cleared her throat and glared at him. "I've never met Efrat, so I can hardly make an identification. Plus, I smell a lot a people in this area, past *and* present."

Ethan looked at Daniel and he shrugged. "I think she's saying we stink."

"I'm not the best tracker. I'll try to pick up her scent and follow it, but I should probably go alone."

"Alone?" Daniel asked. "In the dark?"

Nevia visibly cringed.

"Someone should go with you," Ethan said. "This prison isn't safe when the lights are *on*. If you don't see well in the dark, I don't want you accidentally stepping too close to a cell."

"I'll go," Daniel offered before Ethan could suggest it. "She'd probably smell Cori on you after three showers," he added with a brow lift.

"Good point. Heaton, you're with me. I want to finish checking this floor. I'll radio the guards to do a full sweep and surveil outside. Daniel, if you find Efrat, do me a favor. Don't kill him. I want that privilege."

39

Daniel followed several yards behind Nevia. He didn't want to interfere with her tracking. As much as he wanted to hold her hand in her vulnerable state, he knew it was more important to let her do her job. Cori was once again lost, and it appeared that Nevia was again the only one who could find her.

Nevia seemed to find a strong scent and was following it into the back section of cells where the trial had been held. She didn't seem nearly as concerned with the darkness while she had the scent to follow. It seemed the bloodhound in her was determined to get to the end of the trail no matter where it led.

She crossed by the detained werewolves and made it through the doors leading to the next section without so much as a stubbed toe. Daniel smiled and headed after her.

"Hey!" Callin called over from his cell. Despite the darkness, he seemed no worse for wear. Given his crossed-arm lean on his jail cell wall, he looked like he was just hanging out in his cell, and not really imprisoned by it. "What's going on, healer?"

Daniel let out a coughed scoff at the notion of being a healer. Callin only knew him as the guy who put his finger back on—a noble title for a generous deed, but if he knew Daniel was one of the few people in the world that even a werewolf should fear, he wasn't sure he would get to keep the title.

"Why are the lights out? The lights never go out here."

"Budget cuts." Daniel quipped, but Callin didn't even give him a hint of a smile. He should know better than to joke during a crisis—toughest audience ever. "Efrat has damaged the electrical system, and may have kidnapped Cori." Callin gave him a look that reminded him that he didn't have firsthand knowledge of either of them. "The dude with lightning bolt hands fried the system and stole Ethan's wife," he clarified.

Callin's face lit with concern, but quickly turned to loathing. "Release me and I will help find her."

"Sorry, not my call. I'm just the hired help. Besides, I already got a bloodhound." He glanced over to the door, realizing he had neglected Nevia.

"Please, I owe you a debt."

"Seriously, wolf-man, I'm already Danato's least favorite person in the world."

"Are you immune to electricity?"

"No."

"Then what will you do when you find this man?"

"I figured I'd stand behind Nevia while she waved her gun." Daniel wasn't really concerned about Efrat, but it would be difficult to use his power on someone while ducking bolts of electricity. "You aren't immune either."

"No, but it won't incapacitate me like it will you or your friend. It will just hurt like hell."

"Oh, is that all?" Daniel rolled his eyes and moved to the cell door. "Step back. I'm not sure who the thick one is: me for letting you out, or you for wanting out."

Daniel focused on the lock, and in moments, the mechanism crumbled into ash. He was a good deal cooler, but not nearly cold enough to slow his body.

If Daniel's talent surprised Callin, he didn't share it. He just slid the door open and took the lead, following Nevia.

40

THE CLEAVER SLAMMED DOWN again, and Cori couldn't help but cry out. Efrat had yet to penetrate the ice shell that she had unconsciously formed around her hands and forearm. With every strike, he chipped more ice away. Eventually, the shell would fail and he would reach his target.

The attack on her enraged the house. The floors and walls were creaking, as if they wanted to close in on Efrat to stop him. There was no electricity to light the house, but the fireplace had lit on its own. Judging by the light it was giving off, the flames had to be shooting out of the chimney. She hoped that meant help would be on the way soon.

Even as she closed her eyes to pray for her hero's speedy arrival, a gunshot sounded.

41

"Y OU SHOULD HAVE KNOWN better than to cross me," Frederique said to Nevia's bluing face as she held her off the floor by the neck. They were eye to eye, which left Nevia more than a few inches off the ground.

Daniel was so taken aback by the scene he had walked in on that he didn't react in time to stop Frederique from breaking Nevia's neck. Callin, however, did.

Callin's catalogue-casual male image ripped away when he leaped at Frederique. Daniel wasn't sure he had even seen him move. He was just a breeze and an impact.

Frederique, Nevia, and Callin toppled to the floor. It was not technically the fall that broke Nevia loose, but the bite that Callin put on Frederique's throat. To defend herself, Frederique retracted her attack.

Nevia coughed and gasped for air. Daniel ran to her aid, but she was already crawling away from the fight, flailing her hands in search of something.

Her gun.

"What the hell happened?" Daniel asked just as Frederique shoved—or rather launched—Callin off of her. The man hit the entryway to the section like a ragdoll, but he landed on all fours, positioned like an Olympic track runner. He bounded back at her, and Daniel could only get out of his way.

"Gun," Nevia rasped.

"You can't fecking see, what good does it do you?" he groused at her, but he knew at this point it was going to be a pacifier to her. If he didn't get it for her, she would continue to scramble on the floor in a state of near panic. The absurdity of it all was that she wasn't afraid of Frederique, just the darkness.

42

T HE GUNSHOT WAS LOUD. Cori had been shot and watched several people being shot since she had come to the prison, but she couldn't remember it being so loud. Maybe the house echoed the sound better.

Seeing Efrat's flannel sleeve fray, before soaking with blood, relieved her only slightly. Help was here, and she was certainly safer than she was five minutes ago, but she so desperately wanted that rent in the fabric to be over his heart.

Efrat jumped away from her and out of the line of fire, holding his arm. After he was situated, he pulled her legs toward him, bringing her further behind the island. As he swung her around, she glimpsed her savior before the cabinets obstructed her view.

Belus stood in the entryway. The pistol in his hands was hers. She had never seen him use one, even though he had trained her with it. He seemed rather comfortable with the weapon, but she imagined he would look comfortable no matter what challenge lay before him.

She was happy that someone was here to help her, but a little part of her was disappointed. She would have been much more comforted by seeing Ethan or Danato's face in that doorway. Belus was no doubt brave and clever, and despite his appearance, he was formidable, but Efrat didn't know Belus well enough to be intimidated by those qualities.

Cori loved Belus dearly and trusted him with her life, but in this particular situation, with this foe, Belus was not the hero she needed.

43

DANIEL PUT THE GUN in Nevia's hand and shoved her against a wall. He could see her grind her teeth to keep from saying something scathing about his manhandling and condescension. He leaned in and kissed her, partly to keep things civil between them, and partly because he just really wanted to.

He could tell she wanted to pull away and at one point shifted to do so, but he cupped her cheek to keep her still. He finished the innocent though inappropriately timed kiss with a quick bite of her lower lip—a promise of more to come later.

He rubbed his thumb along her cheek and pleaded, "Please, stay here while I help Callin." He couldn't claim that there wasn't still a glare in her eyes, but she holstered her gun and crossed her arms. She would be content to follow his instructions as long as the lights were out, which was fine with him. That was the only time he really cared about calling the shots, anyway.

Frederique's inhumanly hard nails had already scratched Callin, and his neck showed a laceration twice the size of the one he had inflicted on her. Daniel wasn't sure if anyone could beat a fem-wolf, but Callin was probably as close as anyone would get.

They were both panting, but the only breaks they took were to reposition tactically or ergonomically. Daniel couldn't help Callin if he didn't get away from Frederique, or at least hold still long enough for him to focus on her.

"Do you want some help, Callin?" Daniel asked.

"Stay away, Daniel. I don't want you to get hurt." Callin spoke clearly, despite Frederique's grip on his nether region. Daniel found an even higher level of respect for the werewolf. He was understanding why Ethan had gone out of his way to help him, despite their brief association.

"What about you, Frederique? Can I get you some water, tea... puppy chow?" The insult worked wonderfully. The low growl that erupted from her matched the ferocity of strength she mustered to throw Callin across the room again. The crack that came from his back told Daniel that he probably wouldn't get up as fast as the last time.

Frederique lunged at him. She was a ball of fury with bloody fingernails and a bad hair day that would take a pair of scissors to cure. She had forgotten what he was capable of, or never really understood it. Either way, he was annoyed that he had to teach her a lesson twice for threatening his girlfriend—or whatever she was.

It never took long to focus his energy for the kill mode. In truth, he could disperse a body in seconds. It was not doing it in seconds that took the concentration.

Frederique's body hit a brick wall long before she reached him. The look of shock on her face was familiar. It would have been amusing to him if he hadn't seen it so many times, and if he didn't associate it with so much guilt.

Her body was frozen against that imaginary brick wall, looking at him with wide eyes. She was feeling it now.

The heat.

The friction of every cell in her body simultaneously vibrating.

It wasn't pain yet, at least not any more than stretching one's sore muscles is pain. It was the promise of pain: the pressure before the cut, the bend before the break. He couldn't imagine what it felt like, but if the past was any indication, she now fully understood what he was capable of.

44

"That was a warning shot, Efrat. I'm an excellent marksman," Belus called out from the door. "I owe you that much for saving my life, but that's the only concession I'll offer you."

Efrat had ripped his shirt and cinched his bleeding arm. She remembered he had basic knowledge of first aid, like all well-trained soldiers do. He didn't answer Belus, instead he just threw out a bolt over the island.

Efrat turned his attention back to her hands. The ice was melting on its own. She wasn't sure why. She was in slightly less danger, but not by much.

"I know you don't want to lose your hands," Belus yelled out. Efrat paused, displaying an appreciation for Belus's observation. "I saw the disgust in your eyes. I know you wouldn't willingly handicap yourself, but kidnapping Cori isn't going to get you sympathy. Danato doesn't take kindly to threats against his girl."

"This isn't about gaining sympathy," Efrat yelled back. "It's about freedom."

"We'll never let you go, Efrat, not like this."

"Not freedom from *you*! Freedom from *this*!" Efrat let out a blast that blinded Cori for a moment and left the hair on her head standing on end. "I want control and I don't want to give up my hands to do it."

"How is Cori going to help you with that?"

Efrat looked at her quizzically. The answer he found on her face made him smile. "The rings, Belus," Efrat answered. "Didn't you ever wonder how all this got started? The time-jumping. Jill's memories. It's all because of the rings. She's immune to my power because of them. If they can do that for her, maybe they can contain the power for me."

"This is the first I'm hearing of this," Belus said. Cori could hear the condescension in his voice.

"Belus, I can't take them off! He's going to cut them off! Come in and shoot this—!" Efrat leaped on her stomach, giving her a partial Heimlich maneuver before covering her mouth.

"The doctors will reattach her appendages. She's the only one that can help me!" Efrat yelled in his defense.

"Wrong." Belus's voice was quiet, but he was closer. Cori tipped her head back and found him right in front of the couch, unprotected by barriers, with his gun firmly aimed at the floor. "I'm the only one that can help you."

45

With a degree of difficulty, Daniel released Frederique from his hold. The cool feeling in his body made him shiver, but again, it was nothing to slow his function. The fem-wolf felt the change and took several steps back.

He expected her to continue to retreat with her tail between her legs, but she didn't. She glanced at Nevia, who was still leaning on the wall, though she hadn't managed to keep her gun holstered. When Frederique turned her attention back to Daniel, she was smiling.

"You won't always be there to protect her," she growled quietly enough that Nevia may not have heard it.

"Yes, I will," Daniel said resolutely, even though he didn't really believe he could be.

Frederique stepped forward with the swagger of a woman and, ironically, a cat, all in one. She stopped inches from him, showing no fear of his eyes. She was the third woman that showed no reaction to his abysmal eyes.

He waited for her to offer a verbal threat, but instead she reached to his groin. Fearing what he had previously witnessed of her male ministrations, he moved away. She wrapped her hand around his back to hold him steady and plied tender but firm pressure on him. He couldn't begin to formulate the words he needed to question her, but got out a curse before she pushed her lips to his and forced her tongue into his mouth.

Daniel wasn't the type to push a woman away, but he also wasn't the type to tongue a complete stranger. Well, yes, actually he was that type, but recently he had grown attached to a certain hand in his crotch, and a certain tongue in his mouth, and Frederique didn't belong to either of them.

He offered Frederique a push while he pulled himself free of her tongue. She hardly moved away, but she did release his groin. A bitter-sweet moment, no matter how much he preferred Nevia.

"I won't make this offer again," Frederique purred. "Come with me now and I'll *let* you convince me not to kill your little friend."

Daniel wasn't sure his face could display enough shock for her offer. "Are you bolloxed? I'm not going with a chancer like you."

"I won't promise not to bite, but I will promise not to draw blood." She drew back, taking his hand. "Come now." She glanced at Nevia again, but he didn't dare look. Even if she didn't see them, she certainly smelled what was going on. Frederique's musk was hard to miss. "We can work this out right now, and I won't kill your friend."

Daniel was about to tell her to go to hell, but a thought occurred to him. The simplicity of it was appealing. All he had to do was shag Frederique and he could be Nevia's hero. That sounded reasonable: sleep with another woman to protect the woman you really wanted to be with.

Simple.

"She hasn't stipulated that *no one* would kill me," Nevia chimed in from her wall. He looked back at her and found her gun sloppily hanging over the elbow of her crossed arm. She was looking at the floor, or from her perspective, the blackness that should be the floor. "And she's only offering not to kill me. She might certainly insist on maiming me a little."

Daniel looked back at Frederique, who was practically drooling from the snarl she was baring. Nevia was right, and he was a lecherous fool. He ripped his hand away.

"Let's get one thing straight, Frederique. I don't give a feck about your werewolf politics. I don't care if your retarded second niece rules the council. I don't care if Callin gets his boy or doesn't." He glanced back at Nevia again. "But I do care if she lives or dies. I do care if someone tries to hurt her."

Frederique nodded at him. "So be it," she said without derision. "Better keep her close," she added before walking away.

46

"BELUS, NO!" Cori screamed as best she could under Efrat's clamped hand.

Belus glanced down at her, but didn't attempt to protect himself. "This is your last chance, Efrat."

Efrat's eyes narrowed, baffled by Belus's foolhardy demand. "Chance for what? My future of being an amputee or my future of joining Hirem and Dr. Frank in the afterlife? Neither of them looks very appealing."

Belus shook his head. "No, they don't, but you're the one offering those two options, not us. We've offered to help you, but that wasn't good enough. You had to have more."

"I made that deal for the others. They've resigned themselves to their fate. I haven't—not yet, not while there's a chance." Efrat looked down at Cori with a look that wasn't nearly as sympathetic as it should have been.

Belus chuckled. "You have no chance. In a few minutes, Danato and Ethan will break down that door, and when they see that you're trying to amputate her hands, you won't go to jail. You won't even get a fight, because one of them will break your neck."

"If they can get to me."

"Don't be cocky, Efrat. They will get to you: by gun, by fist, or by pure will, they will kill you." Belus examined the gun in his hand and smiled. "Do you know how long it's been since I've fired a gun? I'm not as eager to pull triggers as some." Belus winked at Cori playfully. It almost brought tears to her eyes seeing his charming side in this of all moments. "I'm offering you a third choice, Efrat. Put down that cleaver and surrender yourself to me. We'll look for options to secure your powers, magical or otherwise, later, but we will look for the options, instead of just locking you away in a box."

"Why?" Efrat growled.

"I think you're on a precipice. To everyone else, you've already fallen over the edge, but you haven't. You're about to, and I think I can stop it. You wouldn't be the first lost cause I've found a path for."

Efrat removed his hand from Cori's mouth and looked her over. "You're just like her. You're living in a fairytale. I can't go back to being the man I was."

"Of course not," Belus said with a hint of condescension. "But being someone else doesn't exclude being a decent human being."

Cori could see that Efrat was contemplating this. She knew this would be a hard step for him. He wasn't the type of man to give up without a fight, but perhaps he was tired of fighting as well. Maybe he could really be a good guy, or at least not an asshole.

Her line of thought stopped cold when he raised the cleaver.

47

"THAT WAS BY FAR the weirdest encounter I've ever had with a female, and I've known some wackos." Daniel helped Callin down the stairs to the infirmary. Nevia had already run ahead to grab a wheelchair.

"Frederique is a typical female werewolf, but she has power, so take that times ten," Callin grunted.

Daniel was pretty sure his back had a few slipped discs; his torso looked off center like a stretched-out rubber-banded figurine. The fact that he was walking wasn't nearly as impressive to Daniel as the fact that he wasn't yowling in pain or weeping, just as any man would, after being thrown across the room by a fem-wolf.

"I get that, but was she really serious about offering herself?"

"Of course." Callin paused to take a labored breath. "She's never met anyone like you before. Whatever you did to her, it scared the bugger out of her. To scare a fem-wolf is like an instant aphrodisiac. Werewolves may walk among men, but we still function by baser instinct. You are powerful, ergo worthy of her. It's sexual submission, as simple as that. Unfortunately, you've also just rejected her, which means instead of burying her head in a pint of ice cream like a human woman, she's going to make it a point to hurt you as much as she can."

"Feck."

Nevia had the door propped open with the wheelchair when they reached the landing. Daniel helped Callin into the chair and Nevia wheeled him into the infirmary, which apparently had a separate generator because it was well lit. He followed behind and waited by the front desk while the nurses took over for her. She said something to Callin before the nurse wheeled him away and he nodded to her.

"What did you say to him?" Daniel couldn't help but ask when she returned.

"Nothing that concerns you," she said, brushing past him. He resisted the urge to grab her arm and pull her back. He wasn't that guy, and she certainly wasn't that girl.

"We should get back to the search," he said, changing the subject.

"I'd like to wait and see if he's okay," she said, sitting down in a plastic chair near the door.

"He's a werewolf, the only creatures predetermined to survive the nuclear holocaust besides roaches."

"It will only take a few minutes. Cori has the entire prison looking for her. I think you can spare five minutes for someone other than your friends."

Daniel looked her over, trying to discern how to approach this mood. Nevia had certainly been mad at him before, but this was different. This wasn't anger stemming from frustration, this was anger stemming from hurt. He had hurt her. It wasn't too hard to figure out how, either.

He cleared his throat and sat across the foyer from her. She was sitting inhumanly prostrate in the chair, but her head was sulking low. He wished he could smell her emotions, so he knew if she was more sad or mad. Not that it mattered. He would have felt just as obligated to apologize for either.

"Look, I know I made a bad choice back there. I know you won't believe me, but I wasn't thinking with my knob. I was thinking about saving you. I was a fool to even consider it. I didn't mean to hurt you."

She lifted her eyes, but not her head. "I'm not mad about that. Breaking up couples is a fem-wolf's favorite game. I wouldn't dream of holding you to a higher standard than other men. Although, I would prefer that you make your best effort to raise your own standards."

"Good." Daniel wasn't sure what to feel about him being held at the same standard as every other man in the world, but he hadn't really earned her expectations yet. He did, however, know how to feel about the word "couple." They hadn't really had the formal discussion on what their relationship status was, but he thought "couple" was a good word to describe them. "Wait, what *are* you mad about then?"

Her breath hissed out, and she rolled her eyes like the thought of having to walk through the complexity of female emotions with him exhausted her.

"I'm not psychic, Nevia. You're going to have to help me out here."

"I'm mad because you have no substance." She paused to offer him room to comment, but he just shook his head in confusion. "I'm prepared to fight for the equality of werewolves. You made it perfectly clear that you don't care about anything, including whether a man gets to be a father to his son."

"Funny, I thought I made it clear that *you* are what I care about."

"Yes, and your friends, but nothing else. You have no desire to fight for anything beyond that small circle."

"How does being loyal to my friends make me a man without substance?"

"Don't you see how different we are? I want to change the world. You're content with it as it is."

He couldn't resist laughing. "Pardon me, love, but Callin getting custody of his son isn't going to ricochet the world into a new era."

"No, but collapsing the Council of the Moon will change the lives of werewolves worldwide."

"Feck, you are tenacious."

"Just figuring that out now?"

"No, I knew you were determined, confident, and insolent. I just didn't realize that you were a spoiled pain in the ass."

"Excuse me." She stood, double-dog daring him to give her an excuse to storm off.

"You heard me." He stood, mimicking her crossed arms. She noted his mockery and uncrossed her arms. "You are so used to getting your way, you can't stand that I'm not falling in line to follow you like your lapdog. You might have more werewolf in you than you realize."

"You remember I'm armed, right?" she said, placing her hands on her hips. She was already losing her footing on superiority. He could tell from her struggle to hold his gaze.

"Go ahead. Pull the gun if it makes you feel better." He stepped closer to her and pulled his glasses off to look directly at her. She wavered for a moment, but conversely to every other person he looked on, she settled her gaze on his eyes and didn't look away.

"I'm not afraid of you, Daniel."

"I know. I'm terrified of you, though." Her brow dipped slightly in question to that statement. "You are a tiny little ball of fire and I want so much to hold you, but you keep burning me."

"What's that supposed to mean?"

"It means I know you want to change the world, but just because I don't, that doesn't mean I'm beneath you. It doesn't mean I'm not good enough for you. If you think it does, then maybe that's our biggest difference of all. I can be a better man for you, Nevia, but I can't be a different man. You need to decide once and for all if that's good enough for you."

Callin cleared his throat from the front desk. He looked none the worse for wear, except for the scratches and bruises. Whatever entanglement his spine was in upon entry, it was now realigned. "Sorry to interrupt, but I would like to continue assisting the search."

"Yeah, sure, man," Daniel mumbled and led the way to the door. He was glad he had a chance to say his piece, but once again he would have to wait for Nevia's response.

48

THE CLEAVER SLICED THROUGH the duct tape painlessly, but that didn't prevent Cori from shrieking. She scurried away from Efrat as she ripped the remaining tape from her wrists. He looked on her with the same distant observation he always did. She knew the slight hint of remorse in his eyes was not from what he almost did, but from the missed opportunity to do it.

"You bastard," Cori snarled, nearly in tears, yet restraining her volume. "You would have done it, wouldn't you?" She got to her feet, and he mirrored her movement.

He scoffed. "I've killed people, Cori, you know that. Why is this so much more heinous to you?"

"Because it's *me*!" She stepped forward to make sure every bit of her volume reached him. "I've saved your ass more than once!" She could feel the ice rebuilding on her hands, and the hair on the back of her neck standing on end.

"Cori." Belus's warning might as well have been to a deaf person because she wasn't about to stop.

"How can you look me in the eye and do to me what you're too proud to do to yourself?"

"We are not friends, Cori!" Efrat screamed back, coming toe to toe with her. His power ebbed around him in a blue haze. "You saved me to satisfy your own conscience. I'm a project for your overstimulated morality!"

Cori could feel the color drain from her face. She was no longer upset, or angry, or scared; she had reached antipathy. She was done. "You're right," she said ever so softly. "We aren't friends." Cori slapped his face. The ice block around her hand was unfortunately gone, but Efrat got the full impact of her hand. He cradled his cheek defensively. She presumed the reaction was to mock her, but the blood streaming through his clamped fingers told her otherwise.

Efrat looked at his bloody hand, appalled. He bore his teeth in a silent snarl and slapped her back. The electricity streaming from his hand wasn't nearly as painful as the impact.

She counterattacked with a fireball that threw him against the wall. He patted out the fire that lingered on his flannel shirt/bandage.

He lunged at her with the same untamed antipathy as she now held for him. She barely got a bolt off before he landed on her, pinning her back to the ground. She could smell burned hair and skin where her hands touched his forearms. He growled, wrenching her hands off and pinning them over her head.

"Stop!" Efrat yelled, breathing hard. "Please." His voice softened and for a moment, he just stared at her. Pain was seeping into his eyes, or perhaps it was just fatigue. "Please stop," he lamented before rolling off her.

She looked at Belus, who had observed the fight with a distant fascination. She couldn't begin to wonder what he thought of her new abilities. She also couldn't imagine what he thought of her not telling him about them. Before she could find out, a slow applause filled the room.

Cori whipped around to look at the door and found General Clark was observing their fight, including her resume of powers. "Well, well, what have we here?" he drawled, looking right at her.

49

CLARK SMILED, BUT IT looked more like a contained sneer. Cori slowly drew herself off the floor. Efrat followed right behind her, his hands ablaze with blue energy. "I thought that whole ice thing was just temporary?"

"Clark, you have no business being here. This is—" Belus started, but Clark didn't even acknowledge the interruption.

"It's not just residual, is it? You have all four elemental powers... and you can wield them."

"Yes, which means you should get the hell away," Cori sputtered, her best tough-girl retort. She might as well have waggled her head and snapped her fingers as seriously as he took it. "Shall I demonstrate?" She held up a hand full of fire.

"Not at all." He drew his gun and pointed it at her. "You've already won me over. You'll be a very nice consolation prize."

"If you lay one hand on her, I will kill you." Belus stepped forward, fuming at Clark, but he hadn't pulled the gun. She presumed it was to prevent unnecessary threat and premature gunfire. That sounded like a logical reason for him to be relying on vacant threats.

Clark looked him over carefully and nodded. "I imagine you would, Keebler." He turned the gun on Belus and fired.

Belus flew back like a victim in a western showdown.

"No!" Cori screamed. She leaped to check on Belus, but Efrat closeted her with his arms. The energy from his outstretched hands created a veil protecting them both. "Belus!"

"This has to stop, Clark!" Efrat yelled at him over her ear. "She'll never be a soldier for you."

"I can be very convincing when I need to be." Clark licked his lips. Cori got the distinct impression he meant torture, but the notable arousal he got from the topic made her back closer to Efrat. It was a strange position they kept getting themselves into. Like a bad marriage, they hated each other, but they still needed each other to survive, so they just kept coming back again.

"You know your bullets are useless, so save yourself the ammo," Efrat warned.

"Not necessarily. Ethan had warned me that you were involved in this little kidnapping, so I switched to rubber bullets." Clark fired the gun again.

Efrat changed tactics from defensive to offensive, but the impact of the bullet in Cori's stomach put them both on their backs. Efrat struggled to uncouple himself from her, while she struggled to figure out how to work her lungs. The gun fired again and Efrat went down. She struggled to move, but the pain and lack of oxygen left her too dizzy to keep her eyes open.

50

Daniel and Nevia trailed behind Callin while he sniffed out Efrat's trail. Nevia was doing her best not to pout, but between his ultimatum and Callin usurping her position, she wasn't hiding it well. At the risk of pissing her off more, he had to ask one question. "I thought your sniffer was better than full werewolves?"

"It is," she snapped before mumbling the explanation. "It's too good. Too many smells. It makes for difficult tracking."

He offered a grunt of acknowledgement and another minute passed in silence.

"I can't change either, you know," she said abruptly, breaking the silence. He glanced at her but remained focused on following Callin.

"I never asked you to."

"I never asked you to change, either. I just don't know what the hell we're doing."

"I thought we were trying to be a couple," he said, using her word.

She stopped to face him, and he did the same. "It's just, I had an image in my head and... you're not it."

"*You* had an image in your head, or your parents put an image in your head?" She didn't seem to like that accusation, but she didn't have a defense. "Look, we've had a two-night stand and one really hot afternoon. If you'd rather scatter than give it a go, I'd rather know now."

Nevia opened her mouth to speak, but Callin once again cleared his throat. Daniel must have given him a rather unfriendly look because Callin held up his hands in surrender. "Sorry, but do you know any reason that Danato would send for a helicopter?"

"Helicopter? This is a no-fly zone. It's kind of part of the whole secret prison thing."

"Then I suggest we get outside, because one is arriving right now."

Daniel glanced between Callin and Nevia a few times before the urgency of the situation settled in. "That son of a bitch," he grumbled before taking off to the nearest stairwell.

51

"BACK SO SOON?" CLEOS asked when Cori came ripping through the crowd. She couldn't fully remember why she was so mad, or at whom, but the uppity bald man staring down his nose at her nearly got backhanded for her lack of focus. "You must be having a bad day."

"Bad life." Cori threw herself onto the sofa, put her feet up on the coffee table, and crossed her arms. A cluster of trophy wives gasped at her audacity. "What?" she yelled at them. "You got something to say?"

Cleos hushed her and sat down beside her. "Easy, Corinthia. They are just pieces of the former women, and certainly not the better pieces. Don't waste your time fighting their hypocrisy. It's all they are."

"I'm supposed to be doing something!" she griped. "Why am I here again?"

"You must be unconscious again. I presume that means you are in danger again... or still."

"Great!" She sank deeper into the couch and tapped her foot.

"May I offer a suggestion?" Cleos pulled a pre-lit pipe from his smoking jacket and puffed on it. She turned slightly to hear his explanation. "You should use this time to figure out a plan."

"I can't figure out a plan! I can't remember what's gone wrong!"

Cleos shushed her again and brushed an errant strand of hair from her face. "The unconscious mind is different from a sleeping one. A sleeping mind is busy reconciling the day's memories. The unconscious mind is like a movie on pause. It's just waiting for the conscious senses to start working again."

"What's your point?" she sniped, and he looked irritated for a moment before proceeding with his explanation.

"What I'm saying is your mind is still fully functional. You just need to get it the signals to jump-start it."

"No shit, Sherlock. I don't suppose you have smelling salts for the brain."

Cleos shrugged. "I could try to find a pathway for you."

"Good, do it." She opened her palm to him.

He chuckled and slid his hand around hers sensually. "Don't you even want to hear my speech about the dangers of cutting new paths in the mind? The leaks I could create, which could cause fractured psyches and personality disorders?"

"No, just get me awake again so I can stop whatever the hell is happening to me."

Cleos sighed and went into her mind. She caught a glimpse of a slide show in her mind. It was as if she couldn't think straight until he found what he was looking for. "There," he said quietly, "that's strange. This seems to be..." Cori peeked her eyes open long enough to see Cleos's crumpled and confounded face. "This is the safest path. It shouldn't interfere with your personality, though you might lose some connective memories."

"Okay, what do I have to do?"

"Try not to get knocked out again. I can't risk doing this twice."

52

DANIEL TRIED TO KEEP up with Callin, but after the gunfire started, it was futile. He looked behind him, but Nevia had fallen behind almost immediately. He wasn't even sure she had taken to running to begin with. That disappointed him. He knew she couldn't possibly hold his friends in as high esteem as he did, but he thought she might put in a little more gumption.

By the time he made it out the doors, the gunfire was getting pretty heavy. Danato and his men were tucked in alongside his house, firing on the men heading to the helicopter. Clark was among them, and one of his soldiers was carrying Cori over his shoulder. Danato's men were doing their best to stop them, but they couldn't risk an all-out massacre with Cori in the mix.

Against the prison wall, close to where Daniel came out, Ethan and Heaton were firing on the men guarding the helicopter that had landed right in the middle of the courtyard. The bullets from both sides were falling short, but they could hardly switch tactics without making themselves vulnerable.

Callin was behind Ethan and Heaton, pacing like a caged animal. He was a man of action, and guns were not likely to impress him, but he did have to abide by basic rules of self-preservation—bulletproof or not, being pummeled by multiple bullets could still put him on the sidelines. He leaned down to say something to Ethan, who was crouched under Heaton, taking the low aim while Heaton took the high.

Ethan looked over at Clark and the bellboy carrying Cori like luggage. He jumped up, knocking Heaton's gun out of position. Daniel started to run over to stop him from doing something stupid, but luckily Callin had the foresight and strength to stop him. Ethan was in the middle of his torrent of emotions when he locked eyes with Daniel.

"Kill him!" Ethan ordered as Daniel made it to him.

Daniel glanced over at Clark, over a hundred yards away. He looked back at Ethan and shook his head. "It's too far, man. I'd kill Cori too."

Ethan was more than disappointed. He was beside himself with fear and anger. They were two emotions that never sat well together. There was no room for patience in that mix. "He's going to take her?" Ethan ground out as Cori was loaded into the helicopter.

"Let him," Callin said more calmly than Daniel would have expected from his first view of the situation.

"What?" Everyone was thinking it, but Heaton asked it.

Callin smiled. "Trust me, Ethan. This fight is only beginning."

Daniel exchanged a look with Heaton, but neither of them knew Callin well enough to know if he was making a plan or just giving Ethan a pep talk. The questions that should have followed were interrupted by the helicopter lifting off the ground.

"Cori!" Ethan ran out to it despite the risk of being shot by Clark's remaining men.

"Shit! Heaton!" Daniel hissed and ran after him.

"I'm on it!" Heaton yelled from behind him.

Ethan didn't shoot as he ran toward the helicopter, but Clark's men didn't offer the same courtesy. Daniel focused on the space between Ethan and the men firing. It was a blanket destruction wave that was easier to do than a focused one, but he had to remain attentive since he wouldn't get a second chance at stopping a bullet.

The coolness filled his body and he could feel his joints ache with the running pace. The guns fired, but the bullets were dust in the wind by the time they reached Ethan. He heard Heaton firing behind them, keeping the left flank by Danato's house off of them.

Daniel didn't even know Callin had run past them until he was ahead of Ethan. The overachieving werewolf took one superman leap at the ascending helicopter. His graceful jump almost fell short when the helicopter veered off toward its destination, but his hand caught the landing skid and didn't let go.

Ethan's shooters gave up the gunfight and ran at him full force. He took down two men with easy punches, but a third got him from behind. A fourth man approached and raised his gun. Daniel threw his contradicting power at him and sent the man forty feet in the opposite direction. Unfortunately, his enthusiastic defense landed him on his ass ten feet away from his previous position.

Heaton came over to check on him. "You okay?"

Daniel gave him a thumbs-up, but he didn't really feel very thumbs-up. Heaton offered him a hand. When he returned to a standing position, he saw a man a few meters behind Heaton about to fire on them. Daniel pushed Heaton protectively to the ground.

The man suddenly fell back, hit by an unexpected round. Daniel exchanged looks with Heaton, who was taking his turn on the ground. Another chorus of gunshots preceded several of Clark's men dropping. They followed the sound and saw Nevia on the roof, taking aim with a borrowed sniper rifle. Naturally, she was getting dead-on shots to the exposed targets.

Daniel smiled as he reached down to return the favor to help Heaton. "Dude, you are so in love with her," he mocked.

"Can you blame me?" Daniel posed coolly, no longer denying the accusation.

"Little help!" Ethan grunted as he tried to fight off four men that had resorted to dog-piling him as an attack.

"Oh!" Daniel and Heaton exclaimed and rushed over to peel the men off with a few well-placed sets of knuckles.

53

Danato watched Ethan and his friends take on the straggling crew by the helicopter, while the others ducked for cover around the house and into the grasses beyond to get away from the roof fire. He couldn't even begin to wonder why Callin was out of his cell, and why he was hanging from the helicopter Cori was being kidnapped in, but he hoped that was a good thing.

For once in his life, he wasn't angry. He was only scared. Cori was too important to him to lose. He didn't care about getting revenge. He didn't care about what he had to do. All he knew was that he couldn't lose another woman he loved.

"Need some help?" Garr said from behind him. Danato turned and found Garr and Remi carefully looped by the arms, observing the situation.

Danato looked at them, wondering how many rules it broke to employ the prisoners for his cause. Then again, if it worked for Cori and Ethan, why not for him? "Yeah." He nodded. "I want these assholes off my property as soon as possible."

Remi smiled and Garr smiled—as best he could. They released each other and marched forward, each with their own agenda.

54

D R. JILLIAN CAME TO inside of a helicopter. She had a vague recollection of why she was there, but it was more like a dream than a memory. Outside the window, a grassy tundra zipped by. She saw a no-name soldier sitting across from her. Beside him was a familiar face: General Clark.

General Gregory Clark was the reason she lost her medical license, and why she had spent the last six years searching for her love. He was the reason she was there. She despised him to her very core.

She had witnessed him kill Hirem. The memory of his death was still fresh in her mind. As was her own death.

It didn't make sense, but it didn't have to. The emotion behind it was raw and penetrating. There was no room for logic at this point. All she could do was wallow in her anger, grief, and fear.

She may not have remembered how she got there, but she knew what she wanted to do now that she was. She was fastened to her seat and her hands were bound behind her, but not the way they should have been. Even now she could feel the anger pooling in her gut, translating to her hands.

She knew she didn't need to fear Clark anymore. She had the power now. She didn't have to leave Hirem's death unanswered for.

55

THERE WERE MOMENTS IN time that just didn't make sense. The first night Ethan spent in Danato's home was the beginning of those moments, but as strange as it was to see a vampire hanging on his bedroom window, it was stranger still to watch Danato directing his men to cover Remi and Garr while they laid waste to Clark's men.

Remi shot blasts of water that lacerated the men. Garr engulfed the high grasses in flames, which scattered the hiding men. Those that weren't taken down by humane leg and arm shots by the prison guards were downed by Nevia. Although she was taking full body shots, their Kevlar vests would keep them alive—just securely unconscious.

Ethan assigned Heaton and Daniel the task of collecting weapons to prevent any further problems. With the good guys back on the winning side, Ethan stared after the diminishing helicopter. His only mode of flying transportation was a dragon, and she wasn't likely to cooperate, nor was Danato. Although, in this particular case, Danato might approve any plan as long as it got Cori back.

Instead, he just put his trust in his newest werewolf friend. He had high hopes that if anyone could save Cori, it would be him.

As he watched, the helicopter wobbled and fire spewed from its cockpit. It careened to the ground along with his hopes of Cori's safe return. A plume of fire and smoke rose above the exterior walls. Paused panic tingled along Ethan's skin, draining his muscle control and making him instantly sick. His knees hit the ground, and he slumped over, unable to make demands on his limbs. The only part of his body that was operating was his eyes. Even with tears welling and blurring his view, he couldn't pry his eyes off the space that the helicopter should have inhabited.

He could hear Danato bellowing at the distant catastrophe with the same anger and pre-emptive grief that he felt, but he couldn't find a thought in his mind, let alone a voice in his throat.

56

D ANATO DIDN'T WANT TO believe the worst. He wanted to believe that Cori was okay. He wanted to believe that the helicopter wasn't high enough; that the drop wouldn't kill her; that she might somehow survive. He wanted to believe, so very much.

"Where is she?" Belus asked from beside him.

Danato glanced down at his friend. Belus looked like he was in pain, and he felt bad that he hadn't gone inside to check on him. His eyes narrowed, demanding the answer to his question without actually saying it.

"She's gone," he answered, not prepared to say the other word until he saw the wreckage for himself.

Efrat stumbled out of the house and triaged the situation. He noticed his fellow elementals working with Danato's men and a grim smile appeared on his face that might as well have been a grimace. Even in the midst of this chaos he had caused, he had the gall to condescend.

Danato stalked toward him intending to rip his head clean off. "You did this!"

"Danato, don't!" Belus yelled after him, but he was already at Efrat's neck.

Efrat grabbed his wrists, sending an arc of electricity through his body that snapped under his fingernails. Despite the pain, Danato didn't let go. He wanted Efrat to pay for everything. Rationally or not, he wanted to blame the last six years on him. If Cori were indeed dead, then there would be no one to care whether he lived or died. He could once and for all rid himself of this pain in the ass.

Several other petitions joined Belus's voice, but no one could grab him since he was as electrically charged as Efrat. Nothing was going to keep him from getting his revenge.

Except perhaps being flung thirty feet by an invisible force.

His connection separated from Efrat and they both landed near each other, but out of reach. Daniel's feet stopped beside him and he stared down at Danato like he was trying to be tough, but remembered that he wasn't. "Don't make me do that again, Danato," he pleaded, more than threatened.

Danato stood up and dusted off his clothes. Daniel fell back, giving him plenty of space. Efrat stood as well. He didn't attack, but his usual embittered facial expression was slightly more sour than usual.

Danato looked at the cluster of people he laughably called his family. They all had the same look. They wanted a leader. Ethan was nearly catatonic with grief. Daniel no doubt would have preferred not to be there at all. Belus was still getting filled in by Heaton, but he was already goading him with wide eyes. They needed a leader, and that leader was him.

"Somebody get me a truck!" he barked at anyone in earshot. "We need to check the wreckage for survivors. Ethan, you're with me. Belus, stay here and monitor things. Get Clark's men rounded up, imprisoned and treated. Heaton can inform the medical staff that they need to prepare for... anything."

Everyone seemed relieved to have an order and jumped to. Belus headed over to check on Garr and Remi's progress. They were starting to have a little too much fun with their herding and would need to be reined in. Nothing Belus couldn't handle.

As he passed Danato, Belus nodded to Efrat. "You should take him with you, too."

Danato would have laughed if he thought he could manage it in his state of paused grief. "What?"

Efrat seemed to be just as surprised by the suggestion and furrowed his brow at Belus.

"He brought me back once." Belus shrugged. "Just in case."

Danato looked back at Efrat. He expected him to smile smugly or outright refuse to help. Instead, he gave a curt nod. "I'll help if I can."

Danato didn't trust him, but there was only going to be two outcomes of this excursion. Either they would find Cori hanging to her life by a thread, in which case they might need a walking defibrillator. Or they would find

Cori dead, in which case Danato and Ethan would fight for the right to kill Efrat.

"Daniel?" Danato didn't take his eyes off Efrat.

"Aye." Daniel moved a little closer.

"You and Efrat are with me, too. He's my medic, and you're his babysitter. If he doesn't behave..." Danato finally looked at Daniel, but he didn't finish the statement. Daniel gave him a slightly sheepish nod of understanding. He may not have liked the unspoken order, but something told Danato that he wouldn't have to ask him twice if it came down to that. At least, in that, Daniel was useful.

57

J ILLIAN ROLLED OFF THE man who had broken her fall. She was bruised and probably had a few dozen micro-fractures that only time could heal, but she was alive. She hadn't intended to be.

The fireball she put through the cabin was enough to take down the helicopter. She was prepared to die on impact, but this man had other plans. He ripped off the door with brute strength and pulled her out before they crashed. He took the brunt of the impact and was, amazingly, still alive, just passed out.

She felt bad that he had risked himself to save her life, especially since she would likely not be keeping it.

She had one goal in coming to this place: to kill her lover. It was a strange gift to offer the one you love, but it was what she owed him for putting him through all of this to begin with.

She walked toward the helicopter wreckage. The fuselage was still burning and the tail rotor was still spinning, but other than that, there was no movement. The bodies inside were charring into unrecognizable blobs, but she knew that one of them was Clark.

They say that revenge doesn't alleviate the pain of loss, and that was true for her. The pain of losing Hirem would never entirely go away, but seeing the man who forced her hand burned to a crisp satisfied her. His death was like a puzzle piece snapping into place. It may not have solved the entire puzzle, but it made the picture clearer.

Now that her job was done, she could finally be with Hirem. She found a particularly sharp piece of the mangled tail boom on the ground. She positioned herself over it and steeled herself for the pain of impaling herself.

She heard the truck pull up and the yelling, but she paid no heed to the name being called or the voices that bellowed it ruefully on the other side of the wreckage. The only voice that caught her attention was Efrat's. She had forgotten about the others. She was so absorbed in her own misery she had left them in this hateful place to fend for themselves.

58

Danato stared into the wreckage at the burning bodies. There was no chance that anyone could survive that. Ethan was kneeling before the blaze, hammering the ground in futile contempt of human frailty. Heaton, the good man that he was, was standing witness, not quite consoling him, but not leaving more than an inch between them.

Danato, on the other hand, couldn't bear to watch Ethan fall apart. It was, unfortunately, an emotion he was all too familiar with. If he had any chance of surviving this pain a second time, he was going to have to stay focused.

He turned away and found Efrat looking down at the ground. He at least had the common decency to look guilty. Danato moved to Daniel, who was keeping one eye on Efrat and one on Ethan. He no doubt would have preferred to be standing by his friend in his time of need, but he didn't dare defy Danato.

He stopped in front of Daniel. They were just far enough from Efrat that he wouldn't hear, but close enough that Efrat would read his body language, so he turned from his view and kept his head down like he was in mourning.

Daniel shifted like he was considering putting a hand on Danato's shoulder, but he never actually did. "Danato..." he started.

"Kill him," Danato said quietly, but with earnest. Daniel swallowed hard, and took in a breath, but didn't move. "Did you hear me?"

"Yeah." Daniel nodded, but he still didn't move.

"Do it now, before he has a chance to defend himself!" Danato hissed between clenched teeth.

Daniel looked back at the prison before answering. "No."

Danato narrowed his eyes and turned to face Daniel full-on. It had been a long time since Daniel had shown so much backbone. It would have been impressive if it wasn't for the timing. "What did you say?"

"I said no, Danato." Daniel puffed up his chest and stiffened his neck, but his so-called scary eyes still wavered at Danato's stare. "You can't imprison me for murder, then hire me to be your hitman."

Danato opened his mouth to explain the difference between torture resulting in murder and self-designated justice.

"Something you need to say to me, Danato?" Efrat asked. He had taken a few steps away from them, but his hands were crackling with energy.

59

DANIEL COULD FEEL THE static in the air. If he rubbed his hands together, he might be able to light a lamp. Danato and Efrat's standoff was enough to draw Ethan out of his agony. Heaton joined the standoff, pulling his pistol.

Ethan didn't bother with any of that. His teeth bared and fists clenched, he ran at Efrat like a football player to a defensive tackle.

Efrat shook his head like he was disappointed. He was about to raise his hand in defense when Heaton chimed in. "Do it and I drop you."

Efrat saw Heaton waving his gun before Ethan bowled him to the ground. For the most part, the fight was fair. Ethan was far stronger, but Efrat was electrified, so it seemed to balance things out.

Ethan got in a few controlled punches before Efrat grabbed him, paralyzing him with pain just long enough to get the upper hand. Then he took his turn to blue Ethan's face. There wasn't much banter except some cussing and the occasional yelp of pain.

When the energy died down on either end, Efrat was pressing down on Ethan's chest, partially strangling him. Danato had moved to stop the encounter, but Daniel and Heaton both had the same thought. They each pressed Danato back. Whether this was about Cori or just comparing cocks, they might as well get it out of their system once and for all.

"You people have no idea how powerful I really am. What I could do to you!" Efrat's voice sounded pinched, like he might be holding back more emotions than anger.

Ethan released his grip on Efrat's wrists and punched him in the face. The solid crack made Daniel and Heaton groan. Ethan rolled Efrat off him, unconscious and bloody-faced. "I'm not exactly using full strength either, shithead." Ethan crouched over Efrat for a moment, like he was considering the same thing Danato had.

"Don't touch him!" Cori yelled from beside the wreckage.

Everyone paused to stare at her, waiting for the mirage to wear off. When it didn't, Ethan was the first to react.

"Cori?" He stood slowly at first, but when he moved, he took his steps in leaps and bounds.

Instead of joining in her lover's running embrace, Cori lifted her hand, palm up, to him. Vines of fire curled along her fingers and formed a ball in her hand. She threw it at Ethan, reversing his approach instantly.

60

ETHAN ROLLED TO A stop near the others. Cori came forward, but stopped by Efrat. She bent down to check his pulse. She examined his face as well. Satisfied that he was alive, she looked back at him.

"You broke his maxilla," she scolded.

"What?" Ethan said, glancing at the rest of them for confirmation that this was indeed a foreign statement.

"You broke his face," she clarified with an eye roll.

"Who the fuck cares?" Ethan said, standing up. "Cori... I thought you were dead." He took a step toward her, but she raised her hands defensively... and offensively. "What's wrong with you? How did you do that?"

"I think you have me confused with someone else," she said and looked back at Danato. "Where are the others, Warden?"

"Others?" Danato asked. He looked just as confused as Ethan felt.

"Remi and Garrett."

"Back at the prison, why?" Danato stepped forward carefully. "What do you want with them?"

"I want to free them from this prison. I owe them at least that much."

"Cori, you don't owe anyone anything," Ethan interjected.

"My name isn't *Cori*," she stated clearly, like that should have been obvious just by looking at her.

"Then who are you?" Danato asked, taking another careful step forward.

"Jillian," a nasal voice said from behind her. Efrat stood, but barely held his ground. Cori rushed back to aid his balance. He looked her over. "Good to see you... Doc."

"Jillian Frank?" Danato clarified. "Cori, why do you think you are Jillian Frank?"

"We need to get the others out. I can't leave you here. I should have thought about the rest of you. I'm sorry," Cori said to Efrat.

"Efrat," Danato threatened, but he ignored him.

Cori put her hand on Efrat's. Ethan felt a pang of betrayal that hurt deeper than when she was visiting Cleos, but he held his tongue, hoping that eventually this story would start to make sense.

"You understand why I did it, don't you?" She squeezed his hand, and he winced slightly, no doubt sore from their bout of fisticuffs. "I loved him too much to watch him suffer. I know he was your friend."

Efrat looked away, hiding whatever reaction he had to that statement. "We weren't much to each other by the time you arrived."

"I searched and searched…"

"I know, Doc." Efrat chuckled and touched Cori's cheek.

Ethan felt Danato shift beside him like he wanted to lunge at them, but Ethan put up his hand to stop him. As strange and uncomfortable as this all was, Efrat seemed to be the only one who knew what the hell she was talking about.

"I don't blame you. I blame that burned bastard, and I blame myself, and…" Efrat looked at Danato. "…and that's it."

Cori looked between the two men, trying to discern this civility. "Efrat, let's go. Let's get you and the others out of here."

"We aren't going anywhere just yet." Efrat brought his attention back to her.

"Why not?"

Efrat took in a deep breath and sighed. "You got your wires crossed, but good this time, don't you, kitten?"

"What do you mean?" she asked.

"When was the last time you touched my hands without getting zapped?" Cori looked down at their touching hands. "What's the last thing you remember, Doc?"

"I broke into the prison to shoot Hirem."

"And how did that go?"

Cori's eyes faded out of focus as she tried to remember.

"You didn't quite manage to shoot him. Someone stopped you."

Cori nodded.

"Then what happened?"

"Clark... he shot me."

61

CORI FELT THE TRANSITION into her own mind like a record suddenly getting on track. She pulled away from Efrat.

"There you go, kitten." He smiled as best he could, but the pain seemed to keep him from being too smug.

She turned and looked at all the confused and askance faces. Ethan's eyes were wide and his mouth was hanging open. He wouldn't get burned again—literally—by his assumptions. "Ethan, I'm so sorry."

He dove at her and lifted her into a bear hug. He swung her around before dropping her suddenly and pulling her away. "Don't you ever almost die on me again! Understand?" The statement was laughable in its context, but his tone was staid. She nodded in agreement, despite having no control over the dangers she might incur in the future.

He hugged her again and pulled her into a luscious kiss that she might have preferred he saved for later. A couple of coughs from Heaton and Daniel broke them up. Cori couldn't help but look at Efrat when they did, just to see what adverse emotion the display might have caused, but he was staring at the rubble that contained Clark. Cori couldn't imagine what he was thinking, but she imagined it was the same thing Jillian felt: relief and satisfaction.

"How did you survive?" Heaton asked.

"Oh, shit!" Cori said. "The werewolf."

"Oh crap, Callin!" Ethan kissed Cori one last time and joined Heaton and Daniel to find the werewolf.

Cori looked at Danato. He hadn't taken his eyes off her since she had arrived as Jillian or herself. He looked blank, like all his colorful emotions had blended to turn him white. She took a step forward and waited for him to speak, but he didn't.

"This…" Cori flipped her hands over to show him. "…is far more recent than you might think. At least my understanding of it is. I thought it was just residual. I didn't know—"

"We can deal with that when we get back to the prison," Danato interrupted her defense. "For now, just give me a hug."

Cori flung her arms around him and he lifted her as he always did, but for a change, he didn't squeeze her too tight. He just held her to him and didn't let her go. He held the embrace so long that she thought he might never let her go, but she didn't even attempt to pull away. Especially since she knew his anger regarding her untold story about her rings was just on pause.

62

"I CAN'T TELL YOU how pleased I am to be joining you in this meeting instead of being treated for my wounds," Efrat snarled after everyone had piled into Danato's office for the ass-ripping of a lifetime. Cori took a seat on Ethan's lap, rather involuntarily, since he wouldn't let her out of reach.

Belus took up a stance to the left of Danato's desk, since Efrat was resting against his usual filing cabinet. Daniel and Heaton were shoulder to shoulder against the wall with their arms crossed. Despite their mismatched features, physically and culturally, Cori couldn't help but think of them as brothers.

"Shut up, Efrat," Danato barked and waved a hand to the door. Nevia stepped in a little bashfully, like she thought she was interrupting.

"The elementals are wondering where they should go." Nevia glanced at Efrat. He rolled his eyes at her, but she didn't seem to take offense.

"We're still figuring that out," Danato said. "Take a seat." He pointed to the open chair. She sat down after exchanging a look with Daniel and Heaton.

"Nice shooting." Heaton winked at her.

"Huh, oh yeah." Danato pulled a stamp from his center drawer. "Well done, Jordan." Danato placed a red-letter stamp *Deceased* across the front of Paul Hirem's file. Cori felt a pang of grief that she knew didn't belong to her, but she felt it anyway. She didn't understand why she kept slipping into Jillian's memories. She assumed her rings were recycling the memories, just as they boomeranged the other powers. What she didn't know, and desperately wanted to, was how to stop it.

Cori glanced back at Efrat to see how he was taking the finality of his friend's life, but he was more interested in palpating his face.

"Does anyone care that my brain fluid is coming out of my nose?" Efrat griped again. He was answered with a semi-synchronized "no" from everyone.

Danato leaned back in his chair and glanced around at each face individually. He stopped on Belus and shrugged. "Fuck, I don't know where to begin."

Belus tried to hide his smirk from everyone, but Cori caught it and couldn't help but smile at the strange timing for him to finally crack open his human side.

"I wouldn't find too much amusement in that, Cori. You've got more check marks than a retard taking a Mensa test," Danato growled, shoving Hirem's file in his drawer. Daniel chuckled, which was a mistake, because Danato opted to start with him.

"Who the hell told you to release a prisoner?" Daniel's mouth opened wide. "The medical staff said he came in with a twisted spine. When did that happen? *How* did that happen?"

"I needed a tracker." Daniel shrugged. "He volunteered."

"He's a prisoner."

"I'm not prejudiced."

"Dude." Heaton shook his head.

"It was my idea," Nevia interrupted before Danato could start yelling. "I couldn't get a lead, and full werewolves are better trackers."

"Like hell it was your idea! I did it on my own," Daniel informed Danato in no uncertain terms. "And it's a good thing, because Little Miss Foot-in-her-Mouth met up with Queen of the Bitches, and nearly got eaten. Callin saved our asses. Well, mostly, I helped, and then it got really weird." Daniel turned to Heaton. "Fem-wolves are always a 'no,' right?"

"Oh, dude." Heaton furrowed his brow.

"I didn't, but she—"

"Daniel!" Belus interrupted. "Would you give Danato a report so we can be out of here by midnight?"

"Oh, right. Nevia and Ethan argued for Callin's release this afternoon. Nevia started a war with the fem-wolves, and Heaton is gay."

"DUDE!" Heaton punched Daniel not-so-lightly in the gut, making him chuff.

Cori looked at Ethan for confirmation, but he was burying his head in her arm to smother his laughter. Danato and Belus exchanged a look that was not amusement.

"I will report." Nevia leaned forward. "The werewolf trial went just as we expected. Callin's case was not even considered, because the council is not interested in changing. The head councilwoman's sister, Leona, is in love with Callin. She is very close to siding with him in his custody battle. Ethan and I took an opportunity to press her a little further in that direction."

"By threatening the head bitch," Daniel interjected. Danato's eyes widened, but Nevia didn't notice since she had turned to "report" to Daniel.

"I didn't threaten anyone. I merely pointed out the werewolf bylaws, something that Leona is no doubt aware of."

"You pointed out that if she was willing to knock her sister off the council, she could get Callin custody of their son."

"Exactly!"

"That's an act of fecking war!" Daniel leaned forward to get in her face. Heaton touched his arm, but didn't make any attempt to draw him back.

"If Leona is willing to fight—"

"It won't be Leona! It will be you, and by extension me and Heaton! You heard that woman! She will relentlessly hunt you until you are dead!"

"Then let her! I've been prepared to fight this battle since the day I found out about my heritage! If you're too much of a coward to fight with me, then walk away!"

Daniel abruptly turned around to face the wall, taking short stuttered breaths to calm himself. Belus and Danato both moved slightly, as if prepared to tackle him if he got out of hand. Heaton shook his head slightly, waving them off, and touched his friend on the back.

After Daniel had calmed himself, he turned to face Nevia. "How many people have you killed, Nevia?"

"I've been using a gun since I was—"

"How many?"

"None."

"Well, I've killed dozens." Daniel looked at Danato. "Most of them in the line of work." Danato tipped his chin up as if he were defending himself against an accusation. Daniel stepped a little closer to Nevia. "Don't you dare call me a coward because I don't want to kill anymore." Nevia opened her mouth to respond, but he interrupted. "And I'm not naïve enough to believe we can survive a fight with fem-wolves without bloodshed."

Daniel looked at Danato. "Are we done here?" He sounded exhausted. "I'd like to get the hell out of here."

Danato nodded. Even if he had more questions, Cori got the sense that he wouldn't have asked him. Whatever animosity there was between him and Daniel, it didn't trump what was going on between Nevia and Daniel.

63

AFTER DANIEL AND HEATON left, Nevia hung around to offer further assistance, but Danato assured her he could manage things. She reluctantly left to pack her things. Cori didn't envy the silent treatment she was likely to get on the long ride from the prison to the train.

After she was gone, Cori slipped into her own chair and prepared for her turn, but it wasn't her turn yet. Danato looked back at Efrat. "Care to offer a report?"

"I'm not sure my report will make much sense to you. Not without a footnote about Cori's choice of jewelry."

Danato looked at her, and she wilted. Now it was her turn. "Obviously I was confused about a lot of things, and details were left out. Until recently, I didn't fully understand what was happening, but I guess my rings are... magical."

"You can touch Efrat when no one else can, and you can make fireballs," Danato specified.

"Yes, but that's not the whole resume. I can absorb the power from others and use it. That's how I found out about Jillian. I accidentally took Cleos's power, and I saw

Dr. Frank's thoughts. I keep tripping over her memories and sometimes I get stuck in them."

"You have Cleos's power still?" Danato asked.

"No, I haven't used it since. The activation seems to be tied to my emotions. I have Hirem's power, Remi's, Garr's, and Efrat's. I can almost wield them all on command now."

Danato rocked in his chair, looking her over, then he turned to Efrat. "Why did you take her? Why, after everything she did to help you, hide you, negotiate on your behalf? Why did you risk revealing yourself to Clark?"

Efrat shrugged. "I thought we could run away together and live happily ever after."

"He wanted my rings," Cori jumped in before Efrat felt too much amusement for his own joke. "He kidnapped and bound me, and since the rings don't come off, he was about to cleave my hands off when Belus interrupted."

Ethan stood up and turned to face Efrat. "You sick bastard!"

"Walk a mile in my shoes, son."

"I could run a marathon in your shoes and still be a better man!"

"Sit down, Ethan!" Belus chided. "You've already had your go at him. We need him intact."

"What the hell for?" he asked before sitting down.

"Remi and Garr have requested amputation of their hands," Belus explained. "They don't want to continue struggling with their handicaps—at least not their supernatural handicaps. Efrat, however, would like to avoid that, so I am going to help him."

"What?" Danato wasn't the only one to say it, but he was the loudest.

Belus looked at him squarely. "I have my reasons. I would rather not make any bold mission statements that I might have to recant later, but rest assured I will take full responsibility for Efrat."

Cori looked back at Efrat. He seemed just as surprised as everyone else, but the fact that he wasn't objecting tremendously was about as acquiescent as he ever got.

Danato scoffed. "Is that it? Does anyone have any more life-altering news? Cori has supernatural powers. My least favorite prisoner—who, by the way, I am not getting paid to house anymore—is going to be mentored by Belus. My best hunting team is probably going to become the most hunted team. A boatload of military men have to be wiped and shipped back to the U.S. with partial amnesia. Not to mention eight fucking months of paperwork to explain this to my superiors!" Danato stood up and leaned over the desk to look at Cori. "All of this because of one fucking key!"

Cori felt Danato's voice booming in her chest, and try as she might, she still couldn't keep back her tears. "I'm sorry I doubted you, Danato. I really am. I just wish things could go back to normal."

"Oh, son of a bitch," Efrat mumbled from behind Cori. It took a moment for her to realize what she had said, but by then it was too late—the wish was out.

64

C ORI FELT THE SHIFT more than saw it. Her rings
burned against her fingers and she felt weightless.
The world blurred like she was about to pass out, but
didn't. When she had gone from sitting in Danato's office
to standing against a kitchen counter with a cup of coffee
in her hand, she wasn't entirely sure.

It took a moment to register the location. The smell
of brewed coffee underlying the affable smell of blueberry
scones took her memory back five years. The woman
washing dishes at the sink hummed an unintelligible tune
that never amounted to a consistent melody, let alone add
up to an actual song. Nevertheless, it was the most pleasant
nonsensical sound Cori could imagine.

She didn't move to her, for fear of bursting the
window into her past. The mug she held, which contained
more cream than coffee, slipped from her fingers—her
mind was too pre-occupied to be bothered with motor
function. The mug tolled on the vinyl floor, but didn't
break.

The humming stopped, and the woman turned
around to see what the commotion was. She looked at the

downed beverage and gave Cori a scolding look. Figment or not, the woman could see her as well. Cori swallowed hard and opened her mouth to say something or ask something, but she never got past the first word.

"Mom."

FELICIA
JEDLICKA

GODS
&
MONSTERS

Book 7
THE WARDEN

Gods & Monsters

Sneak Peek

C ORI HADN'T EXPECTED ANY fewer than three guards with rifles pointed at her head when she exited the semi-trailer. The prison was a high-security facility and took stowaways very seriously. When there was only one armed guard sent to deal with her unexpected arrival, she was a little insulted. Ungracefully, she disentangled her leg from a strip of bubble wrap and smiled at the familiar face.

"Hi, Duke," she said with some relief at seeing anyone she knew from her pre-wish life.

Duke's brow knit tightly before he lifted his rifle for a proper aim. His eyes fluttered over her in examination, but his hands stayed rock-steady with his finger already on the trigger. "Who are you, and what are you doing here?"

"I'm an employee of Danato's, or at least I was. I have to speak to him directly. It's urgent."

"How...? He..." Duke clearly wasn't sure how to handle this. Trespassers were generally wiped by whatever psychic was on good behavior and sent back to their place of origin. Cori already knew too much to simply be whammied and sent on her way. "I need to make a call."

"Please do," Cori said, crossing her arms and looking around like she was merely waiting for her turn in a bathroom stall. The dock manager glared at her through the fog of his cigarette at the far end of the dock. She was certain that there would never be a time or dimensional schism that he didn't hate her and every other human being on earth.

"Miss, what's your name?"

"Cori... Reiger or Pierce, that was never really established."

Duke relayed the information into the walkie-talkie a few more times before the other end stopped asking him to repeat it. She wondered how hard it was going to be to convince Danato that she *was* in his employ, but that she rubbed a lamp and made everyone except her forget it. At least this was one catastrophe caused by honest absentmindedness and not intentional ambiguity. That should earn some points.

"Miss?" Duke said as if he might be interrupting her. "I need to take you to the office." She smiled at him. He always sounded apologetic to her, as if he was sorry that he had to exert anything resembling authority over her. She imagined that his mother had been tremendously exacting in her rules regarding the treatment of ladies.

Duke was torn between letting her lead the way as a ladies-first gesture, and guiding her to the office. Since she already knew the way, but she didn't exactly want to have a gun at her back, she did her best to walk just one step ahead of him. "How have things been here?" she asked when the silence seemed to demand some kind of filler.

Duke nearly lost his balance going up the stairs to the office hallway, but he recovered and nodded at her. "It's been just fine, miss. Thank you for asking." After a short pause, he added. "And with you, miss?"

She sighed. "I accidentally rubbed a lamp, and I completely erased my life here."

Duke stopped midway down the hall and looked at her. She turned to face him. "I'm sorry to hear that. Those wily genies have been a pain in my buttocks as well."

Cori smiled at his reference to buttocks over ass. No swearing in front of the ladies. "Thank you, Duke. I only hope I can convince everyone else as easily as you."

"I've never been much for fibbing, miss, so I just assume that nobody else is either. I've been wrong on a number of occasions, but that doesn't mean I'm going to change my ways. If that makes me a simpleton, then so be it, but I'd hate to miss out on something wonderful just cause I didn't believe it to be true."

"That's a fine way of looking at life, Duke. I respect that, and maybe someday I can learn to be the same. Might keep me out of trouble." She smiled and rolled her eyes.

He smiled warmly, albeit uncomfortably. After a moment, he cleared his throat. "I beg your pardon, miss, but I still have to take you to the office."

She nodded, stifling a giggle. "I know, Duke." She continued down the hallway as he instructed. She was going to have to hang out with Duke more often when she got back to her reality. He seemed like the type of man she could turn to for an honest opinion on just about anything.

Duke knocked on the glass-windowed door before pushing it open and directing her inside. He stayed outside, no doubt to avoid removing his weapon. She expected to see Danato behind the desk, but it was Ethan. She smiled at him, happy that he was here and still him. His hair was shorter, and he didn't smile back at her, but it was him. He lifted out of Danato's chair and circled around to examine her.

"She's unarmed," Duke apprised him.

"Clearly," was all Ethan said in return. "Dismissed."

"Yes, sir." Duke reached for the knob.

"Thank you, Duke," Cori said, since Ethan wouldn't give him any kudos for his performance.

"You told her your name?" Ethan glowered at Duke.

"No, sir, she already knew it." Duke closed the door before any other questions or accusations could be posed.

Ethan approached her and stalked around her like she was a statue he was critiquing for an art show. "Who are you? How do you know about this place? Who sent you?"

"Ethan…" she started to explain, but he clamped onto her face and shoved her head back so he was effectively looming over her.

"Don't toy with me. Whatever your plan is, I will find out. You might as well tell me everything. Who are you?"

"I'm your wife!"

Thank you so much for reading. I hope you enjoyed the ride and if you aren't getting off here, I encourage you to sign up for my newsletter so I can return your generosity with new release updates and special offers.

Sign-Up

You can also find me on Facebook or visit my website. Keep reading!

Website

Facebook

AUTHOR

A s a Nebraska native, and a small-town girl at that, I have very little to occupy my time beyond imagining a world outside of my own reality. By the grace of God and the seat of my pants, I have kept my waning attention span on the task of becoming an author.

So here I am, an indie author, peddling my words in cyberspace and enduring my comeuppances with an unwavering determination. I may not be a professional, and I certainly am not perfect, but if you've made it this far, you have to admit, this smartass yokel does spin quite a yarn.

From the self-inflicted sweatshop conditions of my unairconditioned childhood home, to the arthritis reaping positions of a sedentary lifestyle, I bring to you: my sarcasm, my oddity, and my heart. Take it with a grain of salt or a teaspoon of sugar, but take it for what it is: a story born of the mind, translated to paper, and gifted to you.

I thank you for your readership and even more for your support. Please recommend this book to your friends and family via any social media that you use. Word of mouth is still the best advertising and is greatly appreciated.

Most importantly, keep reading. I'll keep writing.

www.ingramcontent.com/pod-product-compliance
Lightning Source LLC
Chambersburg PA
CBHW011436200726
48289CB00009BA/2783